THE SILENCE IN HER EYES

THE SILENCE IN HER EYES

A NOVEL

ARMANDO LUCAS CORREA

Translated by Nick Caistor and Faye Williams
Additional Translation by Cecilia Molinari

ATRIA BOOKS
NEW YORK LONDON TORONTO SYDNEY NEW DELHI

ATRIA
BOOKS

An Imprint of Simon & Schuster, Inc.
1230 Avenue of the Americas
New York, NY 10020

First Atria Books hardcover edition January 2024

ATRIA BOOKS and colophon are trademarks of Simon & Schuster, Inc.

Simon & Schuster: Celebrating 100 Years of Publishing in 2024

For information about special discounts for bulk purchases,
please contact Simon & Schuster Special Sales at 1-866-506-1949
or business@simonandschuster.com.

The Simon & Schuster Speakers Bureau can bring authors
to your live event. For more information or to book an event, contact
the Simon & Schuster Speakers Bureau at 1-866-248-3049
or visit our website at www.simonspeakers.com.

Interior design by Esther Paradelo

Manufactured in the United States of America

1   3   5   7   9   10   8   6   4   2

Library of Congress Cataloging-in-Publication Data has been applied for.

ISBN 978-1-9821-9750-6
ISBN 978-1-9821-9752-0 (ebook)

For my mother

We don't see things as they are, we see them as we are.
ANAÏS NIN, *Seduction of the Minotaur*

Everything would be performed in front of those eyes.
In front of those unseeing eyes of a dead witness.
YUKIO MISHIMA, *The Temple of the Golden Pavilion*

ONE

On my eighth birthday, the world came to a standstill. My mother's face became a portrait of pain. My father's face vanished forever.

Two decades have passed since then; my mother died on my twenty-eighth birthday. She is now no more than handfuls of ash in a small glass urn, tucked away in a marble mausoleum.

I must have left my white stick in the car, so I am leaning on the arm of Antonia, who has been my constant companion since the day I was born. Others may think I'm blind, but I can see more than they imagine. We are leaving the cemetery behind, with no plans to return. As Mom often assured me in her final days, she won't be on her own, but will be with hundreds of thousands of souls, in a plot close to Heather and Fir Avenues, listening day and night to "Blue in Green." The moment has come for me to fend for myself.

I know the avenues of the cemetery by heart, the plot numbers, the rows of vaults, and the sculptures of angels with downcast eyes looking like exhausted ballerinas. I've visited the century-old Thomas family mausoleum with my mother on more than one occasion. My father rests there too. A decade after his passing, Mom and

I began restoring the place, as if she suspected that another death was around the corner. I never knew which of us she was preparing the space for. I was eighteen at the time and hopeful that my dark days were coming to an end. I was wrong.

It's a short drive from Woodlawn to the home Antonia shares with her husband, Alejo.

"You'll be fine, Leah," she reassures me as she closes the car door. "I'll see you tomorrow. I love you."

The driver continues along the freeway, the Hudson River on the right as we enter Manhattan. In a few minutes, I will be on Morningside Drive, at the limestone entrance of Mont Cenis, the old ivy-covered building where I live. I begin counting the streets, the stoplights, the corners leading to the apartment that is my refuge, my island within an island. A few minutes before arrival, I order my dinner over the phone.

When the car comes to a halt, I thank the driver, take out the folded aluminum white stick, open it, climb the six front steps, and hurry to the elevator. I don't want to run into any of my neighbors or Connor, the building superintendent. The last thing I want is to hear kind remarks or condolences. That will only upset me.

Entering the apartment, I feel a heavy, cold wave of exhaustion wash over me. In the cavernous living room, I open the enormous French doors that lead onto the sliver of a balcony looking out over Morningside Park. The still evening's distant rumble of thunder reaches my ears. A breeze ruffles my hair, but to my eyes the leaves on the trees appear motionless, as though they are struggling against some higher force. On the street corner, an old woman with a dog is looking down at the ground; a man is reading on the bench under the bronze streetlamp; the Columbia University security guard stands at attention like a toy soldier in his sentry box. Nothing moves.

Overwhelmed by the smell of the first raindrops on dry leaves, I pull the doors closed. On the other side of the glass, the old woman and the man have disappeared; the guard is still there, unmoving. A yellow taxi dissolves in a brief instant. For most people, such images are quickly forgotten. For me—a person with motion blindness, or what doctors call akinetopsia—they stay with me, in my mind, like photographs.

When I was growing up, Mom and I shared a ritual of silence. Neither of us ever raised our voices. We knew each other's gestures by heart and picked up on the slightest murmur. My mother grew accustomed to talking to me without moving, her body frozen still. The codes of our language were reduced to verbs conjugated as imperatives: *sit down, walk, lie down, get up*. Those were the orders of the day.

Now I sweep the informational leaflets about akinetopsia—a word derived from Greek that used to remind me of a phrase in the Japanese anime I read when I was a kid—into the recycling basket. And the brain scans and magnetic resonance test results and encephalograms. All gone.

When I was a little girl, I imagined the brain was an enormous worm that expanded to create the different lobes. I imagined the occipital lobe, the visual processing center, wrinkled like a raisin, hemmed in by the parietal and frontal lobes. I imagined how my senses of smell and hearing imposed themselves on the other senses, which gradually lost prominence until they almost faded away altogether.

This is the legacy of having spent two decades monitored by an enormous magnet that tried to read my mind and work out why I rejected movement. I used to dream that a knight in shining armor would wake me with a kiss, but when I opened my eyes, plagued by static images that hung over me like a veil, I regretted those dreams. I knew my life wasn't a fairy tale.

For months, doctors kept me shut up in a Boston hospital, where they meticulously investigated the way I had begun, against my will, to perceive the world. My mother's and Antonia's voices blended in with those of the doctors. "Her speech is not impaired." "Her sense of smell isn't either." "The girl can hear." "She lost her sight," Antonia said to Mom. "She can see a little." The only thing my eyes couldn't capture was movement. At times I thought that everyone around me had died. In the beginning, the sporadic headaches were like someone drilling into my skull, but then they began to disappear as I grew used to them until one day, I no longer felt them anymore.

Antonia kept wondering where the cheerful, vivacious girl that I'd been had gone. In the hospital, the two of them would stand by my bed and talk about me as if I'd also gone deaf. I realized one day that they were whispering. But they did not know that over time, my ears had become more acute and now even the slightest sigh or murmur reached me with the same clarity as elephants perceive the lowest frequencies. I once heard my mom say that my gaze was fading. I began to slowly distance myself from moving figures, those with life, until books became my only friends. I didn't need anything else.

When I emerged from confinement, my mother dedicated her life to my care, tirelessly taking me to consultations with experts, desperately searching for the decisive act that would snap me out of my dream. They explained to her that I was in a kind of visual coma and made it clear that the brain damage was reversible. One day, perhaps in the not-too-distant future, I might regain the twenty-four images per second that the visual field needs in order to perceive movement. *Might.*

Mom became my teacher and I learned to add, subtract, multiply, and divide complex fractions with surprising speed. She encouraged me to be passionate about the far-off worlds and history I could find in the pages of books. Hoping that I would regain the ability to see movement, she refused to have the city's school system, or my doctors, label me as disabled.

Because she was so devoted to me, and because we knew no

one else with my condition, her social circle narrowed. She was an only child like me, born to older parents. She lost her father when she was only twenty; her mother passed away not long after. "You must have children young," she always told me. "If not, you'll leave them all alone at a very early age, like my parents did to me."

Our neighbors, Mrs. Elman and her companion, Olivia, became our family, and Antonia, who has taken care of me since I was a child, bless her, stayed on as my mother's ballast. Though they disagreed on much, they were a good team. Antonia filled the apartment with little prayer cards of the Christian martyr St. Lucy, whose eyes, according to legend, had been gouged out. At night, Antonia would tell me stories about Lucy's sacrifices and how she became the patron saint of the blind on an Italian island far away from Manhattan.

For as long as I can remember, my world has revolved around my mother, Antonia, Dr. Allen, Mrs. Elman, and Olivia. These are the people in my life.

As soon as I hear the intercom buzz, I rush to the door to greet the delivery boy. I have no need of the stick as I make my way down the hall, eyes closed. Opening the door, I wait for him in darkness, surrounded by the smell of sun that always precedes him. The ping of the elevator announces his arrival at my floor, and my heart begins to race. Smiling, I take a deep breath, and when I breathe out again, there he is with my meal—the boy I dream of every night and wait for every evening. He is the boy with the friendly smile and the permanent shadow of stubble, thick eyebrows, long eyelashes, his brow hidden beneath unruly locks of hair he always tidies before meeting me at my door.

When he's in front of my door, I keep my eyes wide open, because I know that if I close them, he will disappear, leaving behind only the aura of sun and sweat he greets me with each day. I want to keep his image.

"Miss Leah, here's your order," he says.

Even though I can't see his lips moving, every one of his words is like a caress.

I stretch out my right hand and he places the bag over my wrist, making sure it doesn't slip. I can feel his warm fingers linger on my forearm.

I mustn't shut my eyes. If I do, he'll disappear, like he always does, I tell myself as a gust of air stings my pupils, the need to blink filling my eyes with tears.

"Call if you need anything else. Have a good evening," the boy says.

I listen to his parting words and hear his voice moving off toward the elevator. Its doors open and close, and it begins to descend; I hear the bell as it reaches the lobby. Then I hear the automatic front door swing closed and the boy's footsteps as he hurries away—but according to my eyes, he is still at my front door, enveloping me with his cheer. Until I blink, and when I open my eyes once more, he is gone.

Walking back to the kitchen, I leave the food on the white stone draining board and go back to the glass doors but don't look out. I think of him staring up at me from the sidewalk, still smiling at me, an orphan now.

And that's when it sinks in. For the first time in my life, I am alone. In this apartment, full of memories. Some of them, I am sure, are better off forgotten.

Mom! I want to call out but find myself unable to. It was time for her to get some rest. That's what I've been telling myself since leaving the cemetery.

I move away from the window, dreaming that the boy is still down below, waiting for an invitation to call on me again.

I lay my supper out on the table: tomato soup, a dinner roll, a pear, and a bar of dark chocolate, half of which I will take to bed with me, saving the rest for tomorrow. On Fridays I usually eat with Mrs. Elman and Olivia, the elderly ladies on the fifth floor, who are as good as grandmothers to me, but this time I made my excuses beforehand, knowing I would be exhausted after the cemetery. Mom had made it crystal clear that she wanted only Antonia and me at her send-off. She didn't want a funeral full of weeping and prayers. And so there were none.

My mother's bedroom is mine now. Tonight, I plan to sleep there for the first time, despite a vague feeling of apprehension that is bubbling up inside me. I worry the hallucinations, which began when I was a teenager, will start up again. In preparation, I've turned the bedroom into a fortress, with walls of books to shield me from noises coming from the adjoining apartment and the voices that tend to float up from the building's interior courtyard. I enjoy my acute sense of hearing in the daytime, but at night it is torture and has grown only more pronounced over the years. That is why, even when the temperature outside is below freezing, I turn the air-conditioning on to block out any hint of sound.

When the sun comes out, the sounds calm down. Daylight softens not only other people's voices, the cries of babies, dogs barking, and the sirens of ambulances going to and from the hospital on the corner but also the sounds of arms slipping into coats, muffled footsteps, and the jagged breathing of the first-floor tenant, who is destined to die of a heart attack if his sleep apnea is any indication.

My sense of smell is another superpower, if you can call it that (I live in New York City, after all). Each of my neighbors has a distinct scent I am able to detect from afar. Whenever I enter the elevator, I can tell if Mr. Hoffman, who smells of mothballs, has recently come or gone, or if the kids from the fifth floor have been messing with the buttons again. I also know if Mrs. Segal's shih tzu has lately wiped its wet muzzle on the rug, or if Mrs. Stein's teenage daughter smoked marijuana the night before.

I go to bed clutching my book and stare at the towering stack Mom left behind for me to conquer on my own. I am currently engrossed in a novel called *A Blind Man's Tale*, by a Japanese author she introduced me to. Mom ordered an English edition from some obscure website, and it took more than two months to arrive. It's about a sightless masseur in medieval Japan who becomes the confidant of a beautiful, lonely noblewoman.

I focus on the words and close my eyes before turning each page. When I open them again, there is the next one. For me reading is a constant process of blinking. It is past midnight by the time I close the book, and I consider turning on some music. Perhaps "Blue in Green," my mother's favorite melody, which my parents used to play every year on their anniversary—they danced to it on their wedding day—but sleep comes quickly tonight.

A scent wakes me up in the middle of the night. It is a subtle fragrance of bergamot, a combination of citrus and black tea. In a second, the masculine scent takes me back to a past I can't define, to my childhood, and terrifies me. I feel like I'm being watched. I think I can hear someone breathing. Am I dreaming?

Still half-asleep, I gather my thoughts and try to piece together a face. The scent is familiar, and yet it doesn't belong to any of my neighbors. This is someone I don't know.

The someone's heart is beating fast. What should I do? Scream? Turn on the light? It must be a nightmare.

In my mind, I go over my bedtime routine. No, I didn't leave the fire escape window open. I'm convinced I locked the front door. There is no cash in the apartment.

So, what could they want? Mom's jewelry? Maybe the laptop? Let them take the laptop. All the possibilities I can think of flash through my mind. *Someone could have followed me home, traced my footsteps, but in that case, I would have noticed right away.* That strange smell I still can't place, a mixture of bergamot . . .

I shudder. A draft of cold air creeps beneath the sheets, sweeps over my body, and settles on my shoulders. I can't stop shivering.

Slowly opening my eyes, I confirm that yes, I am awake. This presence—who or whatever it is—isn't a nightmare. I stay completely still, facedown, and pretend to be asleep.

There is a stranger in the room.

TWO

I hear Antonia open the door quietly to avoid waking me. Every Saturday at eight o'clock, she comes over and bakes bread. The scent of her love floods the apartment. I am still in bed, shaking, my eyes red, when she enters the room.

"Another nightmare?" she asks, opening the curtains to let in what little light comes in from the courtyard.

She sits beside me, takes hold of my icy hands, and tries to rub some warmth into them.

"What's happened to my little girl?" she asks, but I remain silent, my lips trembling.

Then in a rush, I blurt out, "A man came into my room last night."

"What's all this, Leah, are you trying to scare me with your nightmares?"

"Antonia, I was awake, I smelled him."

"Who has a key to the apartment? Only that good-for-nothing super and me." Furious, Antonia stands, raising her voice. "I'm going to speak to him right now."

"It wasn't Connor."

"How can you be so sure?"

"This man smelled of bergamot."

"Of citrus? Of orange?" Antonia sounds annoyed.

"It wasn't cologne; it was mixed with a smell that I still can't put my finger on, and his breath reeked of stale coffee. Connor's breath is always tinged with alcohol, masked with mint chewing gum. And another thing—however much he showers, Connor's skin always smells of nicotine."

"Maybe if you change the locks you won't have these nightmares."

"Antonia, I'll deal with it. Before I go to Book Culture I'll speak to Connor. The lock on the fire escape window doesn't work properly, but I don't think anyone would try to get in from the front of the building. The Columbia security guard is out there."

"What do you mean? Anybody could get in through the fire escape! That guard's always half-asleep. Are you sure you weren't dreaming?" Antonia pauses, concerned. "In that case we should report it to the police."

"Why? So the social workers can say I'm not capable of looking after myself? You know they come to see me twice a month. If they find out I've filed a police report they won't let me stay here on my own, and they'll end up sending me to a home. Is that what you want for me?"

"Leah, they have no power to do something like that. They only come twice a month to help you because of your limitations. It was something your mom agreed to."

I climb out of bed and pause in the hallway before shutting myself in the bathroom; notes of tartness and acidity resonate in my mind. Antonia is still perched on my bed. I know her too well. She is going through all the possibilities: the food delivery boy, who might look innocent on the surface but could be hiding something; the accountant who oversees my trust fund and whom she's never trusted; Connor, a single man, who everyone knows is carrying on with a married woman on the Upper East Side; the pest control man, who somehow seduced the Danish au pair on the second floor.

"You can't keep filling the bedroom with books, Leah. They attract dust and that will make you unwell. However much I clean, I am not a miracle worker."

I listen to her browsing through the books lying open on the bedside table.

"*A Blind Man's Tale?* Why give you this?" she hisses through gritted teeth. "What was Emily thinking, getting you all these books?"

"You know what Mom was like," I call out from the bathroom.

If I inherited anything from my mother, it was her passion for books. Together, we devoured everything that fell into our hands. Now that she is gone, the ones she has left me are my survival guides. Sometimes I think that she was the one who couldn't perceive movement. Her eyes were mine, and time, which stalled for her the moment I hit my head, was a whirlwind for me. I always wanted to be like her, live like her, fall in love with an actor like her, and travel as she dreamed of doing but never could because of me.

"*All the Light We Cannot See, Blindness, The Blind Assassin, The Country of the Blind, In Praise of Shadows* . . . they'll drive my little girl crazy. Oh, Olokun, leave my little one alone," Antonia mutters to herself. I imagine her raising her hands above her head, waving them wildly, as if to ward off the evil spirits she's always feared. She knows that when she moves her hands, she disappears for me.

Since Mom died, Antonia has brought over all her saints, the ones she says she carried with her from Cuba on a boat ferrying lost souls, souls that weighed more than the vessel itself. When I was a child, she told me that if it hadn't been for Elegguá, la Virgen de la Caridad del Cobre, and St. Lazarus, who have been with her since she was born, the sharks would have devoured her in the middle of the gulf when the boat sank. "I closed my eyes and let the waves carry me, let the sea swallow me. After all, I am the daughter of Yemayá, the goddess of the sea," Antonia told me. "When I woke up, I saw a man with eyes more beautiful than a girl could dream. That man, dying of thirst, was holding me. The American Coast Guard was already within our reach. How then could I not marry him? Besides, as a thirty-five-year-old woman with no family in this country, I didn't think I had much of a choice." Since they were both Black, she explained, they settled not in Miami but in New York, where they thought they had a better chance of fitting in.

Along with the saints and virgins, Antonia brought her essences and sacred herbs. "Your papa always listened to me. We'd go to the herbalist together, and I'd prepare him my recipes to get him out of his depressions."

My bathroom is well stocked with amber jars filled with Heavenly Waters from a small store in Brooklyn. Obatalá Rain Water, to bring me peace, clarity, and vision; Ogún Fire Water, for courage, protection, and strength; and my favorite, Oshún Yemayá Ocean River Water, for love, abundance, and fertility.

As a child, I remember Antonia in the kitchen next to a small iron pot of boiling water, mixing colored glass stones, herbs, and dry twigs. I imagined Antonia as some kind of alchemist wanting to transform any metal into gold. When the water was on the verge of evaporating, she would turn off the heat, cover that potion with a white gauze, and let it rest for hours.

When Dad was writhing with headaches, she'd put that warm, damp, white cloth on his forehead. The house would flood with the penetrating smell of a burning forest, and that amber liquid was kept in a glass bottle labeled with a handwritten sign: Do Not Touch.

Once, I saw Antonia let a few drops of that brew fall into the tea she made Dad drink.

My mother initially hired Antonia because she spoke Spanish, and she wanted me to learn the language of Cervantes. She kept Antonia on because she brought love and a sense of order to a house that wasn't always so stable. Mom had studied Latin American literature at Columbia University and even chose my name based on her love for the subject. She and my father decided on Leah, after one of Dad's distant aunts. For my mother it had the added benefit of sounding very close to the verb *to read* in Spanish: *leer*. I would have liked to have been named Emily, after my mother and her mother before her.

Finally, I hear Antonia make her way to the kitchen to prepare breakfast. But before that, I notice the familiar sounds of her moving the living room furniture and lifting up the heavy rug with its soundproof underlay. According to her, evil spirits hide underneath them.

"All this does is hide the dust . . ." I hear her mumble to herself. "My little girl hardly moves around anyway. . . . If her footsteps bother the woman downstairs, she can just put up with it. This is no place for Leah to live."

In Antonia's opinion, it was wrong of Mom to be so protective of me after the accident. "Let her live, let her be independent," she would repeat. "You've kept her captive ever since she hit her head. It's you who has made her blind, when you know full well that our little girl can see us just fine." To be honest, she hovers just as much as Mom, but in her own, more affectionate way.

Antonia has never been able to pronounce the name of my illness. Sometimes she tries to spell it out, breaking down the syllables: a-ki-ne-top-sia. "Could they not have come up with an easier name, so that we humans could say it?" She used to whisper to me that Mom had made the whole thing up. She now understands what it is—a neurological disorder that affects perception—but when it comes down to it, Antonia considers everything around us an illusion. Everyone makes up their own story and, with it, their destiny. "I brought my saints with me when I left my island, and I'll take them with me when it's my turn to pass over to a better world."

I step into the living room with my hair still wet, smelling slightly of cotton and clean water. If Antonia is surprised to see what I'm wearing she doesn't say a word. She is smiling. Sometimes, I like to put on my dad's jackets, his slim, white shirts, and I feel he's with me.

"The hot water has done you good," my dear caretaker tells me.

"It's given you some color back. Look at those beautiful cheeks and lovely lips." She gently cups my chin in her rough hand.

I eat my breakfast standing at the kitchen counter.

"The first thing you're going to do is talk to Connor."

I hug her, give her a kiss, and search the room for my stick.

"Don't forget to wear your jacket. You can never trust spring."

I wink at her. She knows very well I rarely leave the house without Dad's brown wool blazer.

"I can sleep here with you tonight. Alejo is working the night shift," Antonia calls out, so that her voice will reach me at the end of the hall.

"Don't worry. I'll make sure Connor changes the locks today," I reply, and step out the door.

THREE

From the lobby, I can feel Connor's presence outside on the sidewalk. In the first image, he has his back to me, holding a broom; in the second, he is stamping out a cigarette on the ground; in the third he is smiling, his eyes turned toward me, vestiges of smoke still floating around him.

I hear a "good morning" and unfold my stick before making my way down the front steps.

"Hello, Connor. Do you think you could call the locksmith?" I ask without looking directly at him for fear that his image will dissolve. "I want to change the locks as quickly as possible. I only need three keys: one for Antonia, the spare for the building, and one for me."

"I'll have it done this afternoon," he replies with his Irish accent.

Silence follows, then: "You know you can always count on me for anything you need. Especially now that your mom's dead."

It's hard for me to take anything Connor says or does very seriously. He's about my age, a couple of inches taller than me, and wears shorts that reach his knees. He lives alone in the basement apartment.

He once told me that he also likes to read, but he has never spent a single dollar on a book. "What for?" he said. The neighbors leave their discarded ones on a shelf in the laundry room. Sometimes they are detective novels; other times, celebrity biographies. The only thing he doesn't read is self-help books, he insists, because they bore him.

Although his boots are greasy and his shorts are stained and crumpled, his shirts are always ironed, clean, and buttoned all the way up to the collar. He has a buzz cut not because he is balding, he once told me, but because he has naturally curly hair and it's too much work.

I'm not sure how he was ever able to attract a married woman on the Upper East Side into an affair, but if the rumors are true, I'm happy for him that he's got someone in his life.

"Thank you, Connor. Antonia is upstairs. She'll stay and wait for the locksmith."

I continue down Morningside Drive, as far as 115th Street. On the corner, I tap the end of my stick against the sidewalk before crossing. I work out that the nearest car is more than sixty feet away. I keep going, and when I reach 113th Street, beneath the scaffolding of the hospital that is being converted into apartments, I am met by the smell of alcohol, stale sweat, and urine.

"Here comes the little blind girl," I hear someone say. Three homeless people regularly camp out on this block. "By the looks of it, she could do with a good meal. If she carries on like this, a strong wind might blow her away." I smile and say good morning to them, as I always do.

At the entrance to Book Culture on 112th Street, I stand with my face turned toward the Cathedral of St. John the Divine and, as always, let a few seconds pass before opening the door. Now that I've reached my sanctuary, the shock of last night is quickly fading. The first thing I try to do is block my senses, especially smell, so that I can concentrate on reading. The assault of whispered conversations and the mix of odors is disorienting at first, but gradually diminishes once I climb the stairs to my favorite corner. A worn brown leather armchair awaits me, next to the window facing the stockroom. Mark saves it for me every morning, although I like it less now that the new children's section has been set up close by.

I greet him without looking at him, with his long neck, black beard, black acetate glasses, and Irish hunting hat. Whatever the season, he is invariably dressed in a long-sleeved black T-shirt, and his head is always covered, as if he wants to hide. In the first image, Mark is looking at me, surprised, his mouth half-open, as though he wasn't expecting to see me. His heart is racing because he wants to kiss me—or that's what I like to tell myself—and he starts to perspire slightly. In the second image, Mark is embarrassed, his eyes downcast. In the third, Mark is smiling at the blond undergrad who helps out on Saturdays.

"I've left a book on the chair for you," I hear him say in the first image, while I tap the steps to the second floor with my stick, the sound of my Keds hitting the floor with a resounding thud.

Mark is in the creative writing program at Columbia. He's into a lot of things—acting, photography, art, and web design. He was in an experimental acting troupe before he got into graduate school. Now all he talks about is experimental fiction, like *The Raw Shark Texts* and *Invisible Monsters*, books that defy structures and molds. He also loves books about death and is currently obsessed with *The Undertaking* and *Stiff*. He gets excited about clever plays on words and once told me that for him, an idea is no more than the result of a semantic disorder. Each day when I ready myself to leave, which is usually sometime after midday, he comes out with some random quote ("Smash the control images! Smash the control machine!"), never daring to say what I hope he really wants to: *May I walk you home? Take you out?*

Mark is my friend, or at least I think of him as my friend. Or rather, my only friend. Perhaps one day he'll ask me out, for a coffee, but he doesn't dare to; neither do I. He used to sit with me when his shift ended, in silence, yes, distant, and we'd spend hours like that. He would get up from time to time and pick up the books that had been left out of place. I felt he was watching me. At times, it seemed as if he was interrogating me. When I told him about my neurological disorder, he looked me in the eye, as if trying to penetrate my brain, understand my illness, help me. With time, he became an expert on akinetopsia; he spoke to me in scientific terms and even told me that somewhere in the universe there must be a race of beings with the power to not see movement. Mark is restless—he can't stop moving, even though he knows that when he moves, his face becomes a blur to me. He doesn't want me to see his face.

Once, I even dared talk to him about my father. "An actor, like you," I think I told him. In that moment, I didn't tell him that he had died or how it had happened.

It has been a few months since Mark stopped spending time with me. He has taken shelter behind his desk, and he smells faintly of guilt. When he finishes his shift, he sometimes even leaves without saying goodbye. "I've got finals." It seems like he has an exam every day now.

When Mom ended up in hospice, after every time I visited her, I started taking refuge in a corner of the bookstore. Mark would leave me alone. He knew that I suffered seeing my mother lost in another dimension, no longer recognizing me, reacting only to pain.

There have been nights when I've seen him hanging around outside my building. Standing on a corner, then sitting on a bench, under the oaks, like a sentinel. He has never touched me or even shaken my hand. If he wants to give me a book, he sets it aside, as if he is afraid of invading my space, as if I have a contagious disease.

"So *that's* your blind girl who reads," I overhear his coworker say. Never mind that I must be at least six years older than she is. I am sitting in the armchair now, but I can hear them from above.

"Don't tease," Mark says. "She is a perfectly normal girl."

I open my eyes. The three images have vanished. It occurs to me that "blind girl who reads" is the perfect handle for my Instagram profile. It might even work for the stories I want to start posting. Though @anormalgirl might be better. That's what I am in Mark's eyes. No, I'll be @BlindGirlWhoReads.

Now I am surrounded by floating children. Mothers leaning against the bookshelves, some hypnotized by their phones, others holding hot drinks from Starbucks. Someone is breastfeeding, but the image dissolves in a halo of light and crying children.

I set aside the book Mark left for me, *House of Leaves*, adding it to a stack of books I haven't yet read, most of which he's recommended, and which nobody touches even after the bookshop closes. I start to read *A Blind Man's Tale*, picking up where I left off last night, when a child's hand obscures the text. I raise my eyes, but the hand is no longer there.

The voice comes out of thin air.

"How can you read? I thought the letters had shapes or dots, like the ones blind people read by touching the pages."

"Joe! Leave the lady alone! I'm sorry." A woman's voice—I assume Joe's mother.

I close my eyes, and when I open them again the woman is standing in front of me with a pained smile, holding the little boy's hand.

"Don't worry, it's fine. Let's have a look then, Joe: Can you read this paragraph?" I ask.

"Sure I can. I know how to read." The smell of cereal and honey mingles on the child's breath.

"He can't read yet; he's just learning a few phrases right now," his mother explains. She is invisible to me, but her voice is swathed with caffeine, cocoa powder, and talc deodorant. She is making gestures that I can't quite discern.

Joe continues, "One time we saw a blind girl reading a blank book that had little punched dots in it. Yours hasn't got little dots. Your book has real letters."

"Joe, I told you to leave the lady alone."

"But how can she read if she's blind?" the child persists, his voice fading. The image of the child stays on my retinas.

FOUR

Back at Mont Cenis, the third-floor corridor is poorly lit. Connor hasn't changed the bulbs at either end and Mrs. Bemer at number 31 insists on filling the only window with a row of pots of devil's ivy that struggle to survive under the dim light coming from the interior courtyard. She claims she does it to stop people from peeping into her bedroom, where she keeps an electric candle permanently lit on the windowsill.

Antonia argues the plants are there to block the unsightly dent on the copper roof of the basement. If you look carefully, you can make out a silhouette in the metal, made by the body of Mrs. Orman, who either jumped or was pushed out her apartment window ten years ago. Her husband walked free because, according to Antonia, prison isn't made for the rich: "They can always afford the best lawyers, who end up making the victim the guilty party."

A witness testified to having overheard an argument between the two and been about to call 911 when she heard the woman's voice become a scream that shook the building. This was followed by silence, according to the witness. Then a few seconds later, a loud bang. And yet the woman's death was labeled a suicide. Apparently she had a history of mental problems.

I remember Mrs. Orman as a loving, kind woman. When I was a child, she watched me on several occasions, while my mother ran errands. Sometimes I would stay with her in her musty-smelling apartment. Other times, Mrs. Orman preferred coming to our place and we would read together. Her husband, she said, did not like to read and didn't allow any books in their home. At least that's what I remember, along with the perennial pain in her eyes. I was the last one to see her that day. Poor Mrs. Orman . . .

After Mrs. Orman died, I was awakened by nightmares. For a while, I would see myself at the window of her apartment, dizzy and frightened. At least Mrs. Orman is no longer suffering.

"How on earth could Mr. Orman carry on living in that apartment with the imprint of his dead wife within spitting distance of his window? Some folks are plain crazy . . ." Antonia often says.

I find the new key in the mailbox. It is bigger than the previous one and requires more effort to turn it in the lock. But that's okay. If I have trouble with the key, so will an intruder.

Every time Antonia cleans, the smell of the disinfectants, detergents, and alcohol-based products disorients me and brings on a dull pain in my occipital nerve. This time, I can tell she focused on the bedroom and hallway—even the door handle—to purge every last trace of the being, real or imagined, who tormented me. Without smells, sounds become even more amplified; conversations overwhelm me. A symphony of meaningless words, speakers overlapping one another, begins to come from above and below me, from the kitchen windows that open out onto the interior courtyard, where they all jumble up together discordantly:

We're going to put the apartment up for sale.

Do whatever you want. Nothing here is mine anymore. Are you going to put me up for sale too?

We can't keep up with the bills from this place. With the money we save we could live really comfortably.

And when will it end?

Having another coffee? Don't complain to me later.

You down a bottle of wine every night and I don't say anything, so leave me alone. Why do I have to repeat myself every day? Brush your teeth!

Where does the woman who moved in next door to the blind girl get her money from, if she doesn't work?

Why can't you call Leah by her name? The woman who moved in is separated from her husband. The co-op board approved it. I haven't seen her, but Connor says she sometimes leaves the apartment in tears. Poor thing.

I've heard her husband is Michael Turner, a billionaire. He got tired of her. She'd signed a prenup. Silly girl.

Then I hear a low moan coming from the apartment next door. I concentrate, in order to shut out the other conversations, and listen to my new neighbor walking toward the wall we share. The moaning stops, and I hold my breath. I capture the silence.

A person with no scent is not to be trusted. I am convinced that scent is what defines a person's soul.

Until I know what the woman smells like, she will have no face or body to me.

The crying stops, but I know she is still there, perhaps trying to listen too, to find out who lives on the other side of the wall. Nervously, I go to my bedroom, protected by my books, shielded by the cold and the constant hum of the air-conditioning. Before returning to the book about the blind masseur, I try once again to tune into the neighbor's muffled sobs.

I see myself in her: alone in that enormous apartment. The difference is that I can't remember the last time I cried. I haven't shed a single tear since my mother's death. I don't recall having cried at all on the day Dad left this world either. Tears do run down my face on occasion, but they are never caused by emotion. Sometimes, when I keep my eyes open to hold an image in place, I tear up. It's a physical reaction.

After reading for an hour or so, I get up to go to the bathroom and feel an intermittent vibration coming from the neighboring apartment. I switch off the light. The girl must have left her phone in her hallway, and the vibrations are passing along the oak floorboards. I creep closer to the wall, making sure my footsteps don't make even the faintest sound. The vibration stops.

"I told you not to call me again. You're hurting me, don't you see that?"

There is a silence, interrupted by more weeping. I can feel her agitated breathing, her tears, even the woman's fitful shuddering. I can sense the panic that hearing the voice on the other end of the line has provoked.

"Don't even think about coming back. . . . I'll never forgive you for what you did last night. . . . Don't come back here! I've moved on; I don't need you. Just leave me in peace. Don't you get it? There's nothing to sort out. I'm not interested in your money. . . . I'm not interested in anything to do with you!"

I hear her desperation, and I tremble with her, as though the man might harm me too.

"Give me the key. I can't keep moving every two months. Next time I'll get help, from whoever I can find."

I breathe deeply, trying to retrieve the smell of bergamot from the other side of the wall, but it doesn't work. Antonia's disinfectants have erased every last trace. Maybe the intruder last night got the wrong door?

Perhaps he rummaged through the keys in Connor's basement office, and took the key for number 33 instead of number 34? It wasn't me he was after; he was looking for my neighbor.

Now we are both in danger, it seems. A psychopath is putting the whole building at risk. What should I do?

"I'm going to report you!" the voice from the other side of the wall exclaims.

Then I hear the phone bouncing on the wood floor and off the dividing wall. Startled, I stifle a shout, and the girl hears me, I'm sure of it. Or, at least, she stops crying. I sense her hands on the wall, her face, wet with tears, trying to work out who it is on the other side. Could it be him, calling her from the next door apartment? she might wonder. Impossible.

I can feel my neighbor's jagged breathing and, vaguely, smell the scent of tears starting to dry. This allows me, for the first time, to begin to construct a face, although it is still masked by a murky haze. Silence. I can't make out whether the girl feels calm or dread at realizing a stranger has been listening in on her. All I know is that she is still glued to the wall between us.

FIVE

It's Monday morning, and I'm walking to see Dr. Allen. I had planned to cancel my appointment but feared that doing so might arouse suspicion. Ever since my mother went into hospice, I've wanted to reduce my meetings with the neuropsychologist from weekly to monthly. I have no pretext, but I will find one. My mother made it clear with Mr. Baird, the administrator of my trust, that all consultations with Dr. Allen were mandatory. Fortunately, Mr. Baird doesn't seem terribly interested in me. Even though Dr. Allen promised he would never give a negative report about me to Mr. Baird, I'm not entirely convinced. So I go.

Luckily, I slept well last night. With the new lock installed and the reassuring notion that the bergamot-scented intruder was looking not for me but for my neighbor, my fears have lessened. Now, though, before leaving the apartment or going to bed, I make sure to stand in the hallway for a few minutes, then sit on the floorboards, and listen. I didn't hear a single sound from the apartment next door yesterday. Perhaps my neighbor decided to relocate after all.

My phone rings as I round the corner where Riverside Drive meets 116th Street. I know it's Antonia, and that I must answer immediately. Otherwise, she will worry and show up at the apartment or call the police.

"Hi, Antonia. Before you say anything, no one else is going to get into my apartment. You know I've got new locks."

"Leah, I know you can sometimes notice things others can't, my love. It's a gift to help make up for what you've lost. But you also have an extraordinary imagination."

"So you still think I imagined it? If you're so sure I dreamed it, why did you bother to clean the hallway walls, the ceiling, the door handles? Not a single inch escaped your disinfectant. You got rid of every last molecule of the intruder."

"To wipe it from your memory, my love. It's your mind playing tricks on you. Stop thinking, Leah, stop reading, stop inventing stories. But enough about that. I was calling to tell you not to miss your appointment with Dr. Allen."

"Antonia, I'm here, outside his office."

"Tell him your story about the man who got into your apartment."

"He won't come back again."

"What do you mean?"

"Because I heard my neighbor. She left her husband, and he turned up at her apartment on Friday, in the middle of the night. Do you think that's just coincidence? I bet he picked up my key by mistake from Connor's office in the basement."

"Coincidence or not, you should tell the doctor all this."

"I need to go up, otherwise the doctor is going to think I've canceled again."

I'm sick of being treated like a blind girl. Since Mom died a month ago, I've vowed to be independent. I want to get married someday and have children. I still have hope that one day in the future, the damage from the cerebral hemorrhage I suffered when I was eight will be reversed, and I will see the world in motion again.

Dr. Allen's building was designed at the turn of the twentieth century to look like some kind of medieval temple, but no gods or saints are on display. The gothic arches in the dark marble lobby, the impeccably dressed doorman, the porter who operates the elevator with its bronze grille, together make me feel as if I'm going for an appointment in one of Dante's circles of hell.

His office takes up two rooms of a vast family apartment that looks out over the Hudson River and the bland silhouette of New Jersey. The George Washington Bridge is visible in the distance. The receptionist doesn't arrive until ten; as usual, the door has been left ajar for me, the first patient of the day.

The waiting room is a library devoted to the study of the human psyche. The doctor's yellow degree from Harvard University hangs in a corner in a baroque wooden frame with gold detailing, along with his licenses to practice, issued by the City and State of New York.

I know my case is in one of the volumes lining the bookshelves because Mom gave him permission to study and write about me. At first, it was fun to accompany Dr. Allen to his classes at Columbia, answering questions from his colleagues and students. Sometimes they even filmed me doing mundane things like walking around a room, but with endless cables attached to my nerve endings. Sometimes they inserted a device into my pupils that allowed them to see exactly how I perceived the world. But eventually, I refused to go back. I was tired of being treated like a science experiment. Still, Mom continued bringing me to these weekly private sessions in the hope that Dr. Allen would find a cure for me.

The smell of old wood and hair oil snaps me out of these reflections. I close my eyes, and when I open them there is Dr. Allen, wearing dark trousers and a brown-and-green-check jacket. A yellowish shirt and a frayed, gray, knitted tie. Gray hair slicked back, his nose red.

"It's about time, isn't it, Leah? I haven't seen you for a month."

As he settles into his Eames lounge chair, I walk over to the sofa by the window. I stare out at the boats on the Hudson. We both remain silent for several minutes, which is a surprise. He's usually the one to ask the first question: "How have you been?" But today he is apparently waiting for me to begin. I sit and allow more time to pass, entranced by a sailboat that sits motionless in the unmoving waters of the river.

"I've slept in Mom's room for the past three days. I'm more comfortable there, and it's quieter."

"Did you change anything?"

"Of course. I've got all my books there now."

"Just books?"

"What more do I need?"

"Did Antonia help you?"

"Yes, now Antonia is coming more often to help me."

"And the social workers?"

"They'll show up again at some point."

I hear the doctor stand, open one of the metal filing cabinets, and pull out a thick folder. Once a year he submits me to an eye test and brain scans, as if I have a degenerative disease. A label on the cover in capital letters: AKINETOPSIA. He takes out a piece of paper and begins to write. I consider taking out my book and starting to read to help pass the time but decide it's not worth it to rebel. *Be a grown-up.* I think about mentioning the man with the bergamot scent, but back away from that too. I don't want to appear vulnerable.

I would rather tell the doctor that both Mark at Book Culture and the food delivery boy have asked me out on dates; I just can't decide who to say yes to first. Or that I'm getting married next year and plan to start a family soon. But I don't say any of those things. Instead, I keep gazing out at the moored boats.

"I have a neighbor who does nothing but cry," I finally say.

At least that's not a lie. And it might convince the doctor that there are other women out there who are needier, weaker than me.

"Have you met her?" he replies, suddenly intrigued.

"Not yet. I heard her weeping and arguing on the phone with her husband."

"Were you spying on her?"

I laugh and tie my hair back.

"I spend my whole life spying on people. I can't help it. I've just heard your wife, for example. She drenched herself in violet perfume and left the apartment. . . . Ah, and she also put her allergy drops in."

"You never cease to surprise me, Leah. Does it worry you to always be . . . spying?" He hesitates, but his question doesn't upset me.

"Of course not. I've learned to live with it. I listen to what I want, when I want. They're only sounds, often with smells attached. If I concentrate, I can make them out. If I want to, I can hear everything that's going on behind these walls."

The doctor clears his throat.

"Don't worry, I can't read minds yet."

I keep my eyes fixed on the Hudson River and the sailboat.

I take out my phone, focus the image without looking at it, and take a photo. The boat isn't in it, only the choppy waters of the river.

"Do you like taking photographs?"

"I opened an Instagram account."

"What's the name of it?"

"BlindGirlWhoReads."

"Interesting."

"It's not a private account—you can follow me." I know he won't. The doctor lives in another world; he doesn't know or understand social media. "I take photographs from my balcony, of the images I create, before they fade away. But sometimes I'm too late. My phone isn't as quick as I am."

Dr. Allen takes down a note.

"I can look after myself, you can be sure of that."

"I know, Leah, I've always had faith in you."

"I've learned to use sound to measure how far away objects,

people, cars are. I can find my way around much better with my eyes closed than open. I can see things in the dark that no one else can make out. I hear things that are imperceptible to others."

"I'm sure you've grown more independent since your mother was hospitalized, that your abilities have increased. Because you are visually weak, your other senses have become heightened, they've intensified. But I don't need to tell you that. . . . Will you come again next Monday? At the same time?"

"I thought we could see each other every two weeks from now on, or maybe once a month. . . . But no, I'll come next Monday, I promise."

When I step out of the consulting room, the receptionist is hidden behind a heap of files. She smells of hairspray.

On the way out, without turning round, I say quietly:

"See you next Monday." I am confident that she is also trained to hear the softest whisper.

SIX

When I leave the doctor's office, I can smell the storm. Within a few minutes the rain will be lashing down, a cascade of water swirling along Broadway, sweeping away everything in its path. People will be dashing for shelter.

I pause on the corner of Broadway and 116th Street. The passersby appear as static as the Greco-Roman figures on either side, which lead into the Columbia University Campus. I begin counting the seconds as I breathe in the air, laden with signs of the approaching storm. I can sense the traffic lights changing color: green, amber, red, green again. The students quicken their pace when the pedestrian traffic light reaches zero, but I've already worked it out. From that moment, I still have six seconds to get to the other side before the eager yellow taxis burst onto Broadway.

And then the rain comes. I raise my face, still with my eyes closed, and let the cold water caress me. I feel the pleasant sensation of the drops bouncing off my pathetic eyes. I fill my lungs with moist air.

"Let me help you," a student says, taking my arm. I nod, letting the girl escort me along slowly, while the others around us make way for the girl with the white stick.

"Thank you, you're very kind," I say softly.

"You're going to get soaked. Do you live far away?"

"A few steps and I'll be home, don't worry."

I want to be engulfed, to let the rain stream all over me, to be left alone. I walk over to the bronze sculpture of the Alma Mater. Around me I can feel everyone running as though they will melt in the rain.

"Are you lost?" A boy this time, with a Dominican accent.

"No, I'm fine, just enjoying the rain."

The boy bursts out laughing. Perhaps I should put my stick away and open my eyes. That way nobody will interrupt me; I won't appear lost or attract sympathy. But if I do that, I'll end up disoriented and will need a firm hand to guide me back eastward.

Suddenly, someone covers me with an umbrella. I feel the warmth of a body beside me and try to make out its scent but can't. The rain is blunting my sense of smell. Nevertheless, I feel it is someone I know.

"You're going to catch a cold . . ." When I hear his voice, I begin to tremble. The rain has wiped away his smell of sunshine and crowds. It is the delivery boy.

I open my eyes: a girl about to fall down the stairs; two boys frozen mid-leap, avoiding a puddle; a layer of drops, like glass marbles refusing to fall, held still in time and space. In this first image, the delivery boy isn't smiling.

Everyone is running from the rain, but not him. His breath, his sweat, and the rain give his body a subtle, musky scent.

"Would you like to keep the umbrella? I've got class now anyway."

What I'd like is to come with you to your class, and then go and have a coffee together, or why don't you come with me to the bookshop? Or, better yet, to my apartment, where we can dry each other off? Instead, I simply gesture no with my hands, without looking at him. I don't need the umbrella.

A clap of thunder makes us jump.

"Well, good luck. Have a nice day . . ." His voice quickly fades away.

I blink and both the boy and his umbrella have disappeared. Then I see him on the steps, one leg raised to jump two steps at once. I close my eyes and open them again, and am presented with the image of a blurred body with a trail of light behind it, as though it's dissolving. Because of me he got wet, and now he'll be shivering all afternoon.

Using my stick, I quicken my pace like everyone else, and flee the dark clouds crashing down.

I stop when I reach the deli on Amsterdam and 116th Street to order a tuna sandwich and hot chocolate to take home. I consider getting two and asking my new neighbor to join me. Why not? I should show the weeping woman some kindness, alone as she is, abandoned and without any family. It would be good for us to share a meal together.

Back in the apartment building, I climb the stairs to the third floor and stop at the end of the corridor, where the doors of both apartments come together in a right angle: number 33 and number 34.

I take out my key and hesitate. I lift my right hand and feel around my neighbor's door with my index finger, searching for the button of a doorbell I can't locate. I sigh and step into my own apartment. Oh well. I didn't order a second sandwich anyway.

I pull the door closed behind me and turn the key twice in the lock. If my neighbor is home, she must have heard me come in. Leaving my lunch in the kitchen, I stand still in the hallway. Nothing. No tears or sobs today. I am alone once more.

SEVEN

The rain goes on forever. Smells are transformed, and the sound of the rain on the metal air-conditioning unit resonates inside the apartment. The constant noise forces me to move from one place to another, pausing in the hallway, sniffing for smells as if they are ghosts. The good thing about the roar of the storm is that it stifles the neighbors' conversations. Everything is reduced to mere noise, and I decide to make the most of the cacophony by taking on a home project: emptying the walnut sideboard in the dining room.

After Mom, crippled by pain, went to the hospice, where I kept her company day and night for several weeks, I arranged for all the apartment's dusty, old carpets to be replaced and for the walls to be painted a soft, ethereal white. It took several coats to achieve this, to erase the juniper green of the three bedrooms, the gray of the hall, the loathsome yellow of the kitchen, and the dining room's dark ocher. My mother loved color, but I knew she wouldn't be coming back. As it is now, the reflection of light against the walls tempers the sounds. By night, it is easier to take refuge in the darkness.

I also ordered white bedsheets, firm pillows, towels in a warm shade of blue. I changed the china too, as well as the cutlery and glasses: no more gold threads, bouquets of flowers intertwined on antique porcelain. It's all clean and simple. Mom's clothes and shoes went to the basement to be stored until I'm ready to donate them to the Salvation Army, or to whomever might need them most. The only area of the apartment that hasn't yet been tackled is this enormous sideboard.

I open a drawer, pull out a heavy box, and place it on the table, expecting to find family photos or letters. Instead, every item is related to my condition. There isn't a single family keepsake, only a yellowing lace handkerchief in a little box lined with red velvet.

"On Friday I'll take the hankie to Mrs. Elman," I say out loud, in an attempt to shake away thoughts of the past. But first I take out my cell phone and photograph the handkerchief, still in its velvet box. I also record an image of the dark pile of papers sitting on the table.

A lazy breeze wafts through the kitchen, dining room, and living room. The dolls that Mom bought compulsively and that I never played with now sit in a black trash bag that's giving off an unpleasant smell. I have to get rid of it. In another corner, more books are piled up.

I go to the French doors to capture the rain on my iPhone. I'm focusing my silent eyes on the drops clinging motionless to the glass, when I hear the door of number 34 open.

I move quietly out into the entrance hall and try to connect the smells and sounds, searching for the echo of a whimper, paying attention to every step, every movement, analyzing the weight of the body shifting on the carpets, and suddenly I am certain it isn't my neighbor inside the apartment. I try to concentrate again, pushing the sound of rain into the background, and slide down to the floor, against the wall, in order to feel the vibrations through the oak floorboards. I am certain of who it is: it must be the weeping woman's husband, who has come back to look for her. But my neighbor has run away. I wonder if I should shout, call for help, maybe tell Connor.

Thoughts careen around in my head, making me giddy. *Who gave him the right to set foot in the apartment? If the husband pays the rent, perhaps he has a key. That poor girl must feel trapped. What if he has her tied up? That would explain why the apartment has been quiet these last several days.*

I begin to count each time I breathe in and out, holding the air in my lungs for as long as possible. I manage to calm myself, to keep my ever-quickening heartbeats under control.

I hear him step out and lock the door with a turn of the key. I run to my door and stand there, sniffing at the cracks like a desperate animal. I close my eyes and, in that instant, I confirm what I feared: it is the scent of bergamot.

I immediately move away from the door, without making the slightest sound. I am afraid he might smell me, detect the panic crouching behind the metal and wood.

There's no need for me to be afraid. He's not looking for me; there's no reason for him to use the wrong key. And besides, I changed the locks, I repeat to the point of nausea.

I go to the door again. Suddenly, sensing that I am being watched through the peephole, I jump backward, unable to stifle a cry.

Does he think his wife is here with me? Why would she be?

The smell of bergamot begins to seep through the cracks, as though determined to pursue and intimidate me, as though it is trying to whisper in my ear, softly but firmly: *Leave my wife alone. If you don't want any trouble, stop spying on her.*

The imagined voice, mingled with bergamot, penetrates my skin and reaches my nerve endings. I tremble, not knowing how to shake off that faceless presence until I hear him walk slowly down the stairs.

I run to the French doors and pull them wide open. Rain splashes onto the carpet. The guard in his sentry box and a red car are the only images I see. I blink several times, until all I can see is the guard. No sign of the man. He might have gone down to the basement and left through the door that leads out onto 116th Street, making it impossible for me to see his image.

But the scent of bergamot remains at my door.

EIGHT

As time goes by, I have the feeling that those around me are losing their scent. I have begun to confuse the smell of Antonia, of Dr. Allen, of my neighbors. Even Connor's smell has begun to dissolve.

The all-consuming smell of bergamot, together with the sound of the man's weight shifting on the wooden floor, even the speed with which he walked to the stairs, have provided me with enough details to create a mental sketch of my intruder. He is tall and slim, young, long-limbed, with thick fingers and a firm grip. He isn't muscular. I imagine that his hair is thinning. I envision him with a shaved head and a clean-shaven face. I imagine him wearing a dark, possibly black, T-shirt and soft-textured pants. Leather shoes with rubber soles. He doesn't wear a watch or rings, nothing metallic. If I try hard, I might be able to distinguish more, but I am exhausted. I have faith in my senses of smell and hearing, but not in my panicky state of mind.

In bed, beneath the down comforter and with the air-conditioning switched on to full blast, I start to trawl through the images on my Instagram page: the front cover of the book about the blind Japanese man, several sunsets taken from the French doors looking out over Morningside Park, the tides on the Hudson River. The photograph of the water drops on the window glass is ready to be added. I type out "Rain" and upload it.

I need the girl to come back so that I can build a clearer picture; I need a few more sobs, or, better yet, to bump into her in the corridor or the elevator to finish her sketch. I imagine my neighbor with long, dark hair and a pale complexion. Barefoot, wearing a loose-fitting dress, no makeup. I sense that she and the bergamot man are attracted to one another, that in fact they aren't really pushing each other away. He craves her, and she enjoys being desired.

I need to confront the man too, maybe even brush up against him, discreetly if possible. That way I will be able to read him better, find out what he is really after. For all I know, if the girl dies, he might be due to inherit a huge amount of money through some life insurance. What if my nosy neighbors are wrong; what if she is the one who is rich? Or what if the husband lost all his money and is now wandering the streets with no trace of what he once had?

I feel sure my neighbor won't be coming back to Mont Cenis. Maybe that last phone call left her so terrified she decided to run away to another neighborhood, another city, maybe even another state or country.

I go back to Instagram and see that underneath the image of "Rain," I have received my first comment—*you like watching people, don't you*—written by @star32. I click on the profile, but it's blank, with a black circle where the photo should be. The only account they follow is mine, and they have not published a single post. Then come comments from my regular followers:

It's raining here too
What does rain smell like?

Don't go out in that, take care
It's going to rain until Thursday. The weekend will be fair though,
    thank God

We need your selfie

How can you take photographs if you're blind?

Do you live on your own?

The blind girl who sees better than anyone

Why don't you ever post photos of yourself?

Is that East Harlem you can see from your window?

I look back through the comments on my previous posts and don't find any others from @star32 until I get to the cover of *A Blind Man's Tale*. The last comment, recently added, was from @star32: "I'm going to read this book so I can understand you better." I tell myself there is nothing to suggest this is the bergamot man. Anyone could have left a comment like that—there is nothing suspicious about it. I consider blocking them but realize that whoever it is could just set up another account and carry on trolling me.

We all spy on people, don't we? It's only human. There's no reason for me to take it personally.

I close the app, switch off my phone, and try to concentrate on reading. I can't. Sometime after midnight, I see a drop of blood in the neighbor's hallway, as if it is floating, weightless, between the walls. I can see myself, still asleep in bed, nestled underneath my white comforter. Suddenly, the drop of blood starts to spread uncontrollably, covering the wooden floor. Now I am lying in a puddle of still-warm, viscous blood. I look down at my hands; they are blood-stained. I feel my body to check if I am wounded, if the blood belongs to me. Nothing. Not even a paper cut.

I wake with a start.

NINE

The rain continues. My neighbor doesn't return, nor does the berga-mot man. Their outlines begin to fade in my memory. He could have hurt me if he had wanted to, but he didn't. The weeping woman, on the other hand, is a mystery I am determined to solve.

My dream frightened me. If the blood wasn't mine, it must have been my neighbor's. If necessary, I will ask Connor for her name, track her down and go find her. Perhaps she is in danger, has been kidnapped or injured.

It occurs to me I should have knocked on the door when I heard her sobbing in despair. I should have protected her, but it's too late now. My neighbor ran away, and I will have to live with the guilt of neglecting her. I feel responsible for what might have happened to this woman I have never met.

On Friday, I am a little late for Shabbat dinner with Mrs. Elman, and so I run up the stairs to the fifth floor without my stick.

"We were worried. We thought you weren't going to come." Olivia greets me at the door. I hug her before she disappears. She always brings with her the aroma of violet water and cinnamon.

The four apartments on each floor of Mont Cenis all have the same layouts. The two at the end are mirror images of each other.

The two slightly smaller ones in the middle are identical. Mine is a middle apartment; Mrs. Elman's is at the end that faces 115th Street. All of the apartments have views overlooking Morningside Park.

Mrs. Elman's hallway looks narrower than mine because it is flanked on either side by floor-to-ceiling bookcases, filled with leather-bound books with gold lettering. They are covered with layers of dust. I reach the living room; thick damask curtains cover every opening where natural light might penetrate.

In the first image, Mrs. Elman is sitting next to the glass door, her hands a blur because she is constantly fidgeting, as if looking for something or stroking the cretonne fabric of the armchair, her eyes staring into space, with a permanently vague smile on her face. Despite being in her nineties, she still has upright posture, without being rigid. She goes for walks every morning at first light, arm in arm with Olivia, sits to rest on the benches in the park, and contemplates the Boston ivy that is consuming the facade of Mont Cenis.

I close my eyes and step cautiously toward the old woman. Mrs. Elman always smells of forgetfulness. I kiss her cheek and place the lace handkerchief between her wrinkled, liver-spotted fingers, gnarled by arthritis.

"Did it belong to your mother?" comes her sweet, sharp voice.

"It did. I found it and thought of you."

Olivia stands with a steaming dish in the kitchen entryway. In my eyes, she remains there for a few seconds, although I can already hear her walking toward the table.

"Dinner's ready," she says in the first image, the dish looking as if it is about to fall off the table. The steam is solid, stationary. When I blink, Olivia is supporting Mrs. Elman in the middle of the living room. With my eyes closed, I get up and go to the kitchen to get the tray of roasted vegetables.

I hear the sound of the dining room chairs scraping the floor and Mrs. Elman settling in her chair. After setting the tray down, I feel my way to the place where I always sit at the table. From there I can survey the living room, which in the dark looks as though it has been invaded by ivy. The upholstery of the heavy mahogany furniture is moss green; lace tablecloths, rugs, and photographs of Mrs. Elman's family cover every surface.

She, like her late husband, is a survivor of the Holocaust and came to the United States from a concentration camp. They weren't made for each other, she once told me, but necessity incites love. They worked so hard to survive, they forgot to have a family.

Olivia, on the other hand, came from the Dominican Republic and, as she often says, has done nothing in her life except take care of other people's families. She never had children, and never married. She is about ten years younger than Mrs. Elman, though her wrinkles are so deep that they both look the same age. It is hard to imagine what will happen when one of them dies.

I pick up the water jug carefully and fill the glass to my right. I see the liquid, amber in the candlelight, float like a gelatinous mass.

"Here, let me help you," I say, when Olivia sits down with a groan, knocking her glass and spilling water on the tablecloth.

"My hip is killing me," she complains, pressing her fingers on her eyelids and pursing her lips.

"I've said before we should get the doctor to take a look at you," replies Mrs. Elman. I finish pouring the water and begin serving the soup when Olivia snatches the ladle from me.

"Rina, my hip has been hurting since the day I was born. How do you expect it to feel now? Aches and pains only get worse as the years go by."

I keep my eyes closed, their Spanish and eastern European accents wafting over me with a pleasing familiarity. I imagine that one day Antonia and I will be like Olivia and Mrs. Elman, although

Antonia is much older than me. I will have to look after her, and the idea of having someone who relies on me makes me happy.

"Connor mentioned that you changed the locks," Mrs. Elman comments, feigning nonchalance. "He offered to change mine too. But why? Should we be worried here in Mont Cenis?"

"I feel safer with the new lock. I'm on my own now. It felt like the right thing to do." I decide to not tell them about the intruder. It would only frighten them.

"You don't know what this neighborhood was like before you were born. You wouldn't believe all the sinister crimes I saw from the dining room window. There, right before my eyes, in that park, so calm and safe-looking from the outside."

Mrs. Elman's frown softens. "We're protected by the university now. We've even got a guard who keeps watch on the corner."

"Every time somebody new moves into the building, we get rather anxious, but there's no need to worry—this one's a single girl," says Olivia, her eyes narrowing.

"Do you know her? Have you seen her, Olivia?"

I hear the anxiety in my voice and quickly lower my gaze to my bowl of soup.

"The other day we saw her first thing in the morning when we went for our walk. She was standing next to the half-open window, staring out at the park. I waved hello, but she moved back straight-away," Mrs. Elman answers. "Is something wrong?"

"When was that? Have you seen her with anyone?"

"The girl lives alone. She's getting divorced, so I hear," Olivia says. "She's a bit unfriendly, if you ask me. I don't know why she didn't wave back at us."

"She didn't know who we were, Olivia. What must she have thought, seeing a couple of old ladies sitting on a bench, waving their hands about? We could have been waving at someone else in the building."

"It was obvious we were waving at her," Olivia says. "She goes in and out of the building with her head down, as though she doesn't want anyone to see her."

"I think her husband has paid her a visit," I offer quickly.

"How do you know?" This time it's Olivia who is curious.

"I heard a man in her apartment one night," I admit.

"Couldn't it have been a woman? Wasn't it her?"

"It was a man," I say, and then fall silent again.

I put down my napkin and push away my bowl.

"You haven't eaten a thing. If you carry on like that, there'll be nothing left of you."

"You sound just like my mother, Olivia."

"All your mother ever did was protect you," says Mrs. Elman.

"My neighbor is going through a difficult time. I can hear her crying at night. . . . Well, I heard her sobbing one night. And arguing with her husband."

"So you've been listening in on her conversations?"

"Not on purpose. I just hear them. Hers, the people in the apartment above, the neighbors downstairs. I hear everything that anyone says around me—it makes no difference if there are walls, ceilings, apartments between us. . . ." I sigh in exasperation.

"Well, divorce is never easy, is it, my dear?" Mrs. Elman continues.

"How would she know, Rina? She's never been married."

"It seems to me she's asking for help," I say, interrupting them.

"It'll soon be a month since Emily left us," Mrs. Elman interjects quickly, changing the topic.

I must look worried, even though this is how our conversations usually go. If Mrs. Elman and Olivia fail to solve one problem, they move on to another.

"She was on her way out for a long time," Olivia says. "The only thing that kept her fighting the cancer for so long was you, dear girl."

"She would have been happier if they had told her from the start there was no need for me to see more than I do now. I get around just fine even though everything around me is standing still."

"She worried about you—she didn't want people bothering you or hurting you."

"Nobody pays attention to blind girls." I smile, trying to lighten the mood.

"You did the right thing, Leah, changing the lock," Mrs. Elman says. "I think I'll ask Connor to change ours too."

"We don't trust this woman," Olivia thought aloud.

"Why?"

"Because she's so beautiful."

Beautiful. I am even more sorry now that I've never seen her.

After dinner, I read to them as I usually do, and they quickly nod off.

I take the stairs back down to my apartment, and when I reach the fourth floor, I hear someone getting out of the elevator on the third. I stop. It must be either my neighbor or the bergamot man, because the neighbors from numbers 31 and 32 never use the elevator after sundown on Fridays.

I hear footsteps heading to the end of the corridor and feel sure it is the woman, not the man. I take a deep breath, hoping that the slightest hint of a sob or a tear might reach me. I can tell the person is moving quickly. I hear her hurriedly open the door and take refuge inside. When I reach the third floor, the loud clang of the stairwell door locking into place behind me hangs in the air. The elevator door is still open to my eyes, even though I can hear it close; the smell of bergamot is floating out of it. In an instant, I see an arm and worn black leather boots. I close my eyes and concentrate. *Perhaps she is safe now. He's gone, he won't bother us. Was it him?*

I walk deliberately down the hall to my apartment, deciding all is well. As I pass by her door, I sense I am being watched through my neighbor's peephole. I consider smiling, but don't. I go inside my own apartment without lingering by the adjoining wall. I go straight to my room, exhausted.

Tonight at least, no sounds come through the walls.

"Tomorrow I'll go to Book Culture," I tell myself. "Get back to my routine."

I set my book down beside my pillow and fall into a deep, dreamless sleep.

TEN

The sun returns with full force, erasing every trace of the rain, diluting the sounds, and leaving me exposed to the figures that fade as they pass by, like luminous stains. Walking to the bookshop, I am tormented again by the feeling that something terrible is going to happen to the faceless woman next door. What if the bergamot man did mean to harm her last night, which is why she rushed to her apartment? It is up to me to save her, to protect her. I am her witness, perhaps the only one.

I go inside Book Culture and, as always, try to control my senses. The first image I see is Mark, smiling. He almost always drops whatever he's doing when I arrive. In the second, he is by my side, but facing away from me. I use my stick to go up to the second floor.

"You'll be more comfortable today," Mark says, walking beside me on the staircase. "We don't have any kids' activities—nobody's going to bother you. There's just one woman upstairs."

"Thanks . . . I haven't had time to read *House of Leaves* yet," I say, embarrassed.

"Still reading *The Blind Man's Tale?*" he asks. I feel him move to one side so that I can sit down in the armchair.

"Yes," I say. "Still reading *The Blind Man's Tale*. But I'm almost done."

In my mind, I hear him whisper, *I want to read everything you read. I want to see the world like you do.* I imagine I can feel his breath on my neck first, then his tongue.

"I'm thinking of going to Florida," he says.

"Florida?" I ask, surprised by this news.

"To Palm Beach. I haven't visited my grandparents in a while."

He always talks about his grandparents, never about his parents. His parents must be dead like mine. Maybe he wants me to travel with him?

There are customers waiting for him at the counter. He gestures to a girl. The gesture is frozen with me. His arm raised, his body dissolved. The arm is now all that's left of Mark. Blinking, I'm alone.

When I open my eyes again, he is mid-step, making his way back down the stairs.

I check that my stack of books is still in place beside the armchair and keep my eyes closed for a while. When I open them, I see a woman standing at the window. We are alone up here, surrounded by bookshelves. A shaft of light illuminates a tear on her cheek.

Suddenly, I open and close my eyes more than once and a hunch comes over me: the weeping woman is my neighbor, even though this isn't how I imagined her. She is small and slim, like me, but she has ash-blond hair, cut in a pixie style.

She is wearing a purple sleeveless blouse, tucked into loose-fitting black pants.

Expensive-looking dark boots. I stand up and move toward her warily and detect the scent of lavender. When I blink, she is in front of me, looking as though she is trying to decipher me. The tear has dried. Her skin is smooth and lovely. She's wearing lipstick and eyeliner.

"I think we're neighbors," she says.

I turn to search for my white stick, buying time. Now that we're finally face-to-face, I'm not sure what to say. I locate the stick by the side of the armchair. I must look like a nervous wreck. I am.

"Leah, my name's Leah Anderson," I say, my eyes closed. "I live in the apartment next to yours."

"I'm Alice." Her voice is steady. "I moved in a week or two ago. I've seen you leave the building, but I didn't realize you lived at number 33."

With my eyes closed, I pick up my stick.

"If you like, we could walk back to the building together," I say, hoping I don't sound too familiar.

"Better yet, we could have a drink first, maybe a coffee?" Alice replies enthusiastically.

I nod, excitement surging through me. But I wish I had been the one to take the initiative. She's the newcomer, after all. She's the one in trouble.

I can't see Mark anywhere on the sales floor. He's disappeared without saying goodbye.

It's as if Mark has started to vanish.

He must've gotten bored with me.

Alice takes my arm lightly once we get outside, and I lead the way, then stop, eyes closed, waiting for the traffic light to change. We take our seats at one of the tables outside of Le Monde, and both order a café au lait. Alice asks for a croissant as well.

"I saw you crying; that's why I came over. Are you okay?"

"Does that mean you can see, then?"

"There are many types of blindness," I answer.

"You're certainly independent. . . . That must be nice."

Alice's voice is interrupted by snippets of conversation from inside the restaurant, a dog barking, a woman arguing with her teenage son on the street corner. I'm frustrated that I've already lost control of the conversation, but when I open my eyes, I see that she doesn't seem to regard me as helpless, which bolsters my confidence.

"They're going to take a while to serve us out here," I say.

"How do you know?"

"I overheard one of the waiters say that people who sit outside only order coffees; they prefer the customers who sit inside and spend more money on food."

"So it's true that the impairment of one sense heightens others?"

"There have to be some advantages." I smile. I want to add that I can also see smells. But I don't want to overwhelm her.

We're swapping phone numbers when the waiter arrives with our coffees.

"Was there a time when you could see?" she asks.

"I can see, actually. Right now I can see that you're having a coffee. But when you lower your cup and put it down on the table, I keep seeing you with the cup close to your lips, frozen, until I close my eyes again. What I can't see is movement."

I blink again and I imagine Alice shredding her croissant with a surgeon's precision. She leaves the dough and nibbles daintily at the crisp, golden exterior. I want to see every detail, every move. I open and close my eyes constantly so I won't miss the simplest gesture.

I would like to start a conversation with her; I must look nervous, insecure. She must feel uncomfortable. *Alice, we can stay silent as long as you like.*

"They make the best croissants here. Don't you think?" she says.

But neither of us wants to talk about croissants. I'd like her to tell me about the man who torments her.

"Are you all right?" I ask her, and immediately regret it.

I turn around and see a boy watching us. He is beautiful. I smile. I turn back to her, blink, and see a smile on her lips. I close my eyes.

"If you like, we could get together on Monday and go for a walk."

"I'd like that very much," I say.

ELEVEN

"I met her."

Dr. Allen is scribbling notes in his file. I can tell he wants to interrupt me with a question but holds back.

"My neighbor," I explain further. "She didn't say a thing about her divorce, and I ended up talking about my blindness."

"How did that make you feel?"

I turn to capture an image of the doctor: his head is down as he writes, shoulders hunched.

"I told her I could see her."

"And hear through her walls?" I feel his eyes on me now, but the image of him hunched over his notebook remains. I stand up and go over to the bookshelf and take down a volume on akinetopsia.

"Twenty-four images per second, that's all I need. Twenty-four images . . . Do you think I'll be able to see again one day?"

"You can see, Leah."

"You know what I mean. When I was listening to Alice's sobs through our walls, I felt as though I could protect her, that she needed me, but in the end, I always have to blink to get by."

"Why would she need you?"

"Don't you get it? She's obviously going through something. She had been crying when I saw her in the bookshop. I'm sick of feeling that everyone has to help me, that people feel sorry for me."

"Nobody feels sorry for you. Could it be that you feel sorry for yourself?"

I suddenly feel light-headed, and slump back into the armchair, my breathing ragged.

"If you like, we can continue next week," Dr. Allen says.

"Alice is really scared. There were a couple of days there when I thought she was okay. But I don't think she is. She's just putting on a brave face."

"And what can you do about that?"

"I don't know, but I have to help her."

"Does she know you live next door, and that you can hear her conversations?"

"She knows we're neighbors. . . . I made it very clear that I can hear everything happening around me, no matter how far away. I thought she'd be shocked. But she was interested. In me. It was nice."

My phone vibrates. I check the screen. It's a message from Alice: *See you sometime after midday?*

I put my phone away and suddenly regret sharing all of this with the good doctor. I'm a grown woman, and I don't need his input when all I want to do is get to know my neighbor better, to offer her the protection she clearly needs. To be her witness when something goes wrong. At least now I know that Alice is all right physically. I didn't see any signs of abuse during our time together the other day, no cuts or bruises. She clearly wasn't kidnapped during the days her apartment was quiet. Nothing was as bad as I had imagined.

"You should be more careful."

"In what way?" I reply.

"You shouldn't be eavesdropping on distant conversations."

"I've already told you I don't eavesdrop."

"Alice might feel harassed."

"I expect that, from now on, Alice will be careful about what she says, and where she says it." I stand and replace the book on the shelf.

"You can borrow it, if you wish."

"I know all there is to know about akinetopsia. What good would it do me, reading about my own limitations?"

Silence. Dr. Allen is measuring every word I say, just like the images that freeze in my mind.

"I've been writing lately," I say, feeling daring.

I do not rush to blink, to see his reaction. But I'm sure he's smiling.

"Sometimes I hear voices. It's as if my mother were dictating what I write," I say.

"I think it's great that you're writing. You are an excellent reader— you must also be a good writer."

"It's a love story. A girl, a boy . . . It's my story."

"Does this mean you've met a young man?"

"It's fiction. But I'm the heroine. Her name is Leah."

"And can the Leah in your story see?"

"She cannot see movement. As the narrator, I am the one who guides her. Someday I hope to publish it. Maybe I can post it on-line."

Session finally over, I pick up my bag and unfold my stick. I wish I could take the stairs, but since Dr. Allen's office is on the sixteenth floor, I wait for what has got to be the slowest elevator in the whole city. I hear the chime of the bell as it stops on each floor until the noisy grille opens in front of me. Inside: the elevator operator, head down, pressing his hand on the controls; a woman with white hair wearing a string of pearls; a sweaty, unshaven old man tugging at his pet's leash. I hear barking, but the dog is a bright white cloud that I can't make out because it won't stop moving. My presence has unsettled it. His owner pulls him back when he pushes his muzzle toward my legs, but the dog keeps at it, determined to catch my scent. I feel him fussing around frantically at my feet. Never once do I see him.

TWELVE

I leave the apartment building for my outing with Alice with my hair still wet from my bath. I wanted to freshen up after my appointment with Dr. Allen. It's a gorgeous day out, sunny. A gust of wind lifts my thin, blue cotton dress. I decide against using my stick, and once on the corner use the sounds around me to get my bearings. I cross the street toward Morningside Park with my eyes open and sit down on one of the benches that face the building to look at the balcony doors of the two neighboring third-floor apartments: Alice's, with its original 1905 molding, and mine, with the new wooden panels that Mom had fitted a few years earlier, after the building was lashed by a storm that flooded lower Manhattan. Alice and I agreed to meet in front of the building, and so I wait. I feel anxious.

With my eyes still on the third floor, I nearly miss seeing Olivia out on the sidewalk, most likely headed for the market. She probably waved at me on her way out, but all I catch is a snapshot of her as she's turning the corner, her back to me, heavy-legged. I hope she's not in too much pain.

The next thing I see is Alice standing near the security guard's hut. Then she is in front of me near the bench.

"Have you ventured into Morningside Park yet?" I ask.

"No, I haven't. Let's do it," she says gamely and takes my elbow. I catch a refreshing whiff of lavender soap.

We take the steep steps down into the park. After every few, Alice stops momentarily, reassuring herself, it occurs to me, that we are not being followed.

"Shall we sit down somewhere? Get a bite to eat?" she asks.

"Follow me," I say.

Every corner of Morningside Heights is engraved on my memory. Every building, every bump in the pavement, all of the spots where the homeless people congregate that Mom always warned me about. I remember going down those steep, sunken stairs, which seemed endless to me, on Dad's shoulders. Together we became an invincible giant. We hid behind the trees, speaking extra softly so that not even the ants could hear us. We battled imaginary enemies, shadows, and wild animals that proliferated at night in the park. Then, with Mom, it was different. The park no longer contained enemies to battle. Now I only had to learn how to overcome obstacles. "When I was little, my mother used to tell me our neighborhood was the boundary between danger and safety. The park is the dividing line," I say.

"Does the light bother you?" Alice asks.

"I get around better in the dark."

"In the dark?"

"Here's the thing: in a movie there are twenty-four images per second; that's how you perceive movement on-screen. I can record only one image at a time. I prefer to walk with my eyes closed. It makes things difficult when your eyes hold on to one image even after everything around you has changed."

After making our way through Morningside, we soon reach one of my regular haunts, Cafe Amrita, just north of Central Park, and are seated in the back of the dining room area, where it's quiet.

"How long have you suffered from it?" Alice asks me.

"Since I was eight," I say, then pick up my menu. "I think we should order before the café gets too full. This place will be packed with students before long. The paninis here are really good."

"I'm sorry. I hope I'm not making you uncomfortable, asking questions. Or boring you."

"No, not at all. It's nice just to talk to someone my age. I normally run with a slightly older crowd," I joke. When she looks at me curiously, I clarify: "I mean, besides my housekeeper, Antonia, who is in her sixties, I spend time with Olivia and Mrs. Elman upstairs. Mrs. Elman is in her nineties. Olivia is younger, but not by much. I love them. They're like family to me."

"Yeah, I know what you mean. My husband is older than me, and we mostly spend time with his older friends and their wives. I can't tell you how refreshing it is to talk about something other than real estate, charity functions, and their plastic surgeons' vacation schedules." She smiles. "How old are you, anyway?"

"Twenty-eight," I say.

"We're the same age! I thought you were younger than me for some reason. My advice? Never get married. It ages you."

Sitting opposite her with my back to the restaurant, I notice the stillness of Alice's body. She has a broad, clear forehead, her short bangs swept over to one side. She's wearing small river-pearl earrings. A fine gold chain rests on her delicate collarbone. Her full lips are tinted with a pale red gloss. Her eyes, though, are a blur.

"By the looks of it, you come here often," she says.

"Always with my stick. Seeing me walk in with you with my eyes open has caused total confusion. The boy behind the counter just asked the waitress if I got my sight back."

"You're joking!" Alice laughs.

I see Alice's face relax into a warm expression and try to hold on to this image of my new friend.

"I looked up akinetopsia on Google," she continues. "Your problem is one of perception."

"Like I said, the thing I can't see is movement. Right now I can hear you, I can sense you, and if I look down"—I look down at Alice's hands—"your arms are a translucent stain. I can make out your body, because you're sitting still. You see the bus going along the avenue?" I point out to the street. "I can only make out the front; the rest of it is a multicolored trail of light."

"Your eyes work like a camera that captures images as though they were taken at a slow shutter speed, and the slightest movement means they start to disintegrate. But when you look at something that is still, do you see it out of focus?"

Alice is talking like an expert.

"Don't move," I say, with my eyes closed. I wait a few seconds and can feel Alice holding her breath. "You can breathe, but don't move at all. Not even a blink."

I open my eyes and see hers in detail for the first time: her eyebrows are light brown, far apart, and her eyes honey-colored, but red as if she has been crying or didn't sleep well last night.

"Have you been crying?" I dare to ask.

I blink, and when I open my eyes again, I see Alice has turned her face away from me, as if she's embarrassed.

"I have been afraid of dogs since I was a child," I offer. "Now I'm terrified of bees."

"I totally get it. A dog around you that won't stop moving; hearing a bee buzzing around you, not knowing where it's going to land."

"What about you? What are you afraid of?"

I hear Alice exhale loudly, as though trying to decide how to answer. I am certain that if she only confesses her fears, she will feel a great weight lifted and, with my help, be able to face them. I silently will her to tell me the truth, not to evade my question.

"My husband. The only thing I'm afraid of is my husband, Michael."

THIRTEEN

As Alice and I are walking home along Morningside Drive and going past the Cathedral of St. John the Divine, I recall my adolescence, when I spent my mornings wandering the neighborhood with my mother and, sometimes, Antonia, who introduced me to the half-built church garden, which to me was like a labyrinth. I learned to recognize every exotic shrub that grew there. I decoded new smells, gave them meaning. I made mental notes that I later wrote down when I got home. They were like school trips for me.

"Penny for your thoughts?" Alice asks.

I hesitate to answer. Now that I've gotten her to open up a little, I don't want our conversation to revert back to me. But maybe this is how it works: I share with her, then she shares with me.

"This walk makes me think of my mother. I lost her two months ago." I shake my head. "Not lost, exactly," I add. "I mean, she died."

"I'm so sorry, Leah."

"We took this walk together so many times. At least she's at peace now, listening day and night to 'Blue in Green.'"

"'Blue in Green'?" Alice asks, puzzled.

"Her and my dad's favorite Miles Davis tune. They're both buried near his tomb now. They live near him in the cemetery."

As we near Mont Cenis, Alice stops dead. An ambulance is parked in front of the building, its emergency lights flashing. Many of our neighbors are outside, and two police cars are blocking traffic. I feel Alice's arms embrace me. She buries her face between my neck and right shoulder. I can feel her ragged breathing and wonder how best to console her, or why she requires consoling before we even know what has happened. Is it possible her husband has something to do with this? I rub her back gently.

When I open my eyes again, I see the ambulance, along with a group of paramedics, and Connor in the distance. *Is she afraid of Connor?* But I cling to that image, widen my nostrils, and pick up molecules of ether, alcohol, and a cold, sweet substance. I focus my mind and begin to make out jumbled dialogue:

The poor thing.

She was very old.

Is she dead?

Maybe someone killed her to get their hands on her money.

Oh, the things you come out with . . .

Well, you never know these days.

"Who looks after her?" a police officer asks.

"She didn't have any children," Connor says. "She only has Olivia, but as you can see, she's just as old as Mrs. Elman. Oh, and the neighbor from number 33. She's not old, but she can't see."

The voices continue.

Did you know her?

A grouchy old woman.

There's always an ambulance around here. Every week they take some oldie away on a gurney.

Close your eyes, don't look. Is there blood?

I told you not to look!

She had a heart attack, maybe a stroke.

That building's cursed. I'd rather die than live there.

Then I feel something like a punch in the chest. It is hard to breathe, as if the people around me have taken all the oxygen. Mrs. Elman is being carried out on a gurney, unconscious. The last time I saw her, I don't remember if I said goodbye to her with a hug and a kiss. Mrs. Elman was already very old, so old that she was a burden to Olivia, even though they didn't see it that way. Olivia will be fine. Poor Olivia. Poor Mrs. Elman.

FOURTEEN

Mrs. Elman died in the early hours of Tuesday morning, alone in her hospital room. The doctor waited until dawn before notifying Olivia. There will be no funeral. Mrs. Elman left instructions on what her headstone should say, and money for the burial. She arranged it so that Olivia could stay in the apartment until the end of her days. After that, it will be passed down to me.

"I was able to give her a kiss before they took her away, but they wouldn't let me dress her as she deserved. She went in an old, faded housecoat." Olivia is rocking slowly in an armchair; I'm listening to her with my eyes closed. "When did you last see her?" she asks.

"We had supper on Friday, remember?"

"Oh yes. You know she loved you like a granddaughter. Your mother was always her favorite, but after she died, it was you."

"I know, Olivia. We're going to miss her so much. You need to get some rest now."

"Rest from what? I haven't moved from this armchair since they took her away. Little by little we're being abandoned. Now all that's left is to wait for the end. We all have an end."

More than Mrs. Elman's paid companion, Olivia became her only family.

"You'll have to come and have supper with me on Fridays now," she adds, getting up for a glass of water. "Though we can do it any other day of the week, if you'd like. You're not getting away from me."

"Of course not."

Between sips, she says: "I saw that you went out with her."

"Alice, her name is Alice."

"Do you know something?" Her accent is thick with fatigue. "There is something about her I don't like."

"Alice is going through a difficult time, Olivia. That's all."

"You can't go through life with tears in your eyes," the old woman says, wagging her finger in the air. "That woman wants people to feel sorry for her. Marriages begin and end, that's just life."

"You're being very harsh. You've only set eyes on her a couple of times. You don't know her at all," I protest.

I think about Alice's hug when we reached the ambulance, the way she leaned on me.

"And you think you really know her?"

"We've talked. She doesn't know anyone in the building."

"And what's she doing whispering in Connor's ear?" Olivia shoots back, clearly trying to sow doubt in my mind.

"When did you see her with him?"

"One night I saw her coming in, and then she left about an hour later. She stood waiting outside for a few minutes until Connor arrived. I saw them talking as though they knew each other."

"Did you actually hear what they said? No. You saw them from the fifth floor. Besides, all of us talk to Connor. He's the super. I hope she was asking him to change her lock. That would stop her feeling so afraid."

"What's she afraid of?"

"Her husband."

"The husband again!"

"She's running away from him, Olivia! She came to this building to escape him, and now he won't stop harassing her."

"Her husband has never been to visit her here," Olivia interjects with conviction.

"How can you be so sure?" I ask. My hands are sweaty; I wipe them on my dress.

"I've never seen him come in or leave the building. You know I spend all day sitting on the balcony."

"I don't think you're able to see everyone who comes and goes from up here on the fifth floor. And besides, how would you even know what he looks like?"

"Well, you can't see properly at all," Olivia fires back.

It's time for me to go. I give her a hug and quietly make my exit.

"Do you want anything from here? Something to remember Mrs. Elman by?" I hear the old woman call out to me down the stairwell.

"No, but thank you, Olivia."

●　●　●　●

"It's awful not to say goodbye to someone," Antonia says to me the next day, while she cleans. "That's the most terrible thing about death, not saying goodbye."

"Olivia was with her until she lost consciousness," I correct her.

"Poor Olivia. The two of them relied on one another. What's going to become of her now?"

"We'll still have supper together every Friday."

"One supper a week won't soothe her grief, Leah. I'll go up and spend some time with her later on."

"We should try to get her to hire someone to help her."

"Hmm, you know what Olivia's like. She'll look after that apartment until the very end, until she's taken out on a gurney, like Mrs. Elman. She's so stubborn."

I try to read but can't concentrate; the sound of the vacuum is taking up all the space in my head. All I have left now are Antonia and Olivia. But there's Alice too, I remember.

FIFTEEN

With the living room in darkness, I open the door to the balcony and try to conceal myself in a corner, but I can't seem to get away from the amber light of the century-old streetlamp anchored across the street. The scene in front of me is shadowy, like a badly painted fresco; the wind is blowing.

If I had been the one to see Alice and Connor talking outside, I would have been able to make out their conversation. From now on, if I'm going to protect Alice, I need to know where she is and what she's doing.

I look down from the balcony to the side entrance that leads straight into the building's basement, with the black automatic disabled-access door, which I have always refused to use. I see Connor there every night, taking a smoke break, watching Columbia students pass by.

No doubt he finds Alice attractive. Why wouldn't he? Alice is a rare beauty. Maybe she's his mysterious Upper East Side lover and fled to Mont Cenis to be near him. I laugh out loud at the absurdity and close the glass doors. I blame Olivia for unsettling me with her suspicious talk. Alice is my friend. Poor Connor is a good if simple-minded man. I resolve to set aside these ridiculous ideas and have a seat on the living room sofa.

This time of night, I can hear all the residents of Mont Cenis absorbed in TV shows and conversation. Laughter and commercial announcements come to me in an elongated echo. I close my eyes and let myself be carried along by the spiral of sound coming from the apartment above:

If you don't make up your mind, I'll do it for you. I'm sick and tired of waiting.

Can't you see what you've become? You're useless!

It's the sound of furniture moving. The Phillipses must be rearranging the living room. Beth is the one doing most of the work; Larry is still in the recliner. They've been married for years, childless.

What's become of us? I hear her sobs grow increasingly shrill, full of reproach. Larry doesn't reply, no doubt weary of the unrelenting battle. I hear him get up. Then the music begins. A chorus of male voices gives way to a woman singing:

Into each life some rain must fall . . . But too much is falling in mine . . . Into each heart some tears must fall . . . But someday the sun will shine . . .

As always, the music wipes out their conversation. I imagine the Phillipses giving up their differences and dancing to the rhythm of that old song.

I sit down to write. I haven't written a word in a while. The laptop has been closed, sitting there in the corner of the dining room table. I open it. I look for the folder named "A normal girl." There are five thousand words written. I start to read but I have no energy. I keep thinking about my neighbor and I close the computer.

On my way to my bedroom, I hear Alice through the wall: she isn't alone.

I hear multiple steps, and someone drops a bag on the floor. I sense a man taking off his jacket, letting out a sigh. I still can't recognize the voices. They mumble, they don't want to be heard.

I try to communicate silently with Alice through the wall.

Are you okay? Tell me if you need me. You only have to knock. I'm here. Is it your husband? Did he force his way in?

I glue myself to the wall, desperate to smell every pore of the dividing line between us. I scurry noiselessly to my front door and am about to open it to inhale the molecules the man would have left outside, when I hear a murmur. Why are they still in the entrance hall? Why not move into the living room?

"Alice?" I whisper.

I imagine the man with his hands around Alice's neck, choking her. I picture her pleading with him before going limp and surrendering. But no, I can tell they're still standing at some distance from each other. Alice is closer to the wall than he is.

I must concentrate harder. I carefully open my apartment door and step out into the corridor. The light of the overhead strips is blinding, so I keep my eyes closed.

Come on, get to work! I scream out to my senses. As I reach my hand out to the door handle of number 34, I begin to pant. *No. It isn't Connor; it's the bergamot man. And Alice opened her door to him. No one forced his way in.*

I pause for a moment, and then slam my front door with a bang. The vibration resonates in my feet and I stand still for several seconds. Alice must have heard it. She now knows that I am home and can hear everything. I will keep her safe. I'm here if she needs me.

Back inside my apartment, I raise my palm to the wall and slide it along to find exactly where they must be standing. I must absorb every sound wave. I listen as they move away toward the master bedroom. As my nostrils begin to burn, I make a conscious decision to ignore every smell. I wait for a cry for help, a sob, a sign of desperation.

I can sense how the man is gripping Alice's back, and how she is allowing herself to be taken. They say nothing to each other. His mouth is on hers, on her neck, her breasts, then farther down between her legs. The image of the two of them begins to fade as I move away from the wall.

Perhaps Olivia is right: I don't know Alice at all. Two coffees and a stroll around the park, listening to her cries through the wall, has told me nothing about her. Defeated, I head to my bedroom. I struggle to stay awake and eventually fall asleep burdened with doubts.

Past midnight, I am woken by a crash. I run to the dividing wall in the hallway and fling myself down on the hardwood floor. I can smell Alice's anguish on the other side.

"What's happened? Do you need help?" I ask one question after another, in a desperate burst.

I have her right there; she is practically whispering in my ear. Alice has been thrown to the floor.

"Alice?" I insist quietly, but loud enough so that she will hear me through the wall.

I imagine the man's hand, covering Alice's nose and mouth, then he allows a gulp of air to reach her lungs.

Alice's voice reaches me, weakly: "Everything's fine. I'll see you tomorrow."

"Alice!" I shout.

"Leah, I'll see you tomorrow." Her voice is no more than a sigh.

I hear two people rise at the same time and move to another room. I stay curled up on the hall rug for the rest of the night, waiting for another bang, another fall.

There is no doubt. My friend is in danger.

SIXTEEN

When the intercom buzzes, I look at the time on my phone: 9:45 a.m. The social workers are early. The day after Mom died, two social workers came over and said they would visit me again. I've been postponing the appointment week after week. I wish Antonia were here today. I'm determined to make the best impression possible.

Unfortunately, I didn't sleep well last night; my face looks strained, and my eyes are red. I'm dressed already, but I run to the bathroom and sprinkle cold water on my eyelashes for good measure. I stand in front of the mirror; the water looks like clear gelatin splattered across my face. I have to trim my bangs or they will fall over my eyes. Every time Antonia sees me in front of the mirror, she tells me I am beautiful. When I was a child, she used to tell me I had the face of an angel. I don't want to have the face of an angel. I'm not. As I move away from the mirror, the angel remains in the reflection of the glass. I am the other one.

I hear the elevator open on my floor and walk in time with my visitors so that I will be at the door when they knock, warm, convincing smile at the ready.

I greet Sharon and Julia with my eyes wide open, risking a barrage of images, voices, and smells, but it takes only a few steps until we are sitting down in the living room, them on the sofa, me in the armchair closest to the French doors. If I start to feel dizzy, I will do my breathing exercises.

I can't make out any details on the faces of the women, who smell of vanilla, apple, and roses. I close my eyes and one of the women, in a sickly sweet tone, says to her colleague: "As you can see, Leah is coping really well by herself, don't you think?"

I smile and acknowledge the compliment with a slight nod.

"Do you miss your mom?" she continues. "Well, of course you do, how could you not miss her? Does Antonia still come by every week?"

They already know the answer to that. They called Antonia and Dr. Allen before coming here.

"Mom left everything well organized," I say obediently.

"It looks like it," Sharon says. "Mind if I use your bathroom?"

It's the classic social worker trick, a way to snoop without coming across as invasive. I show her the way.

"The only thing we care about is helping you to be independent."

I don't reply. I am concentrating on the social worker's movements in the corridor. If she goes into my bedroom she will see the piles of books stacked up against the walls and no doubt check to see if they are appropriate reading material.

She returns with damp hands, which she touches to her cheeks. Maybe she's hot. "Shall I open the balcony door to let in some fresh air?" I ask, the perfect hostess.

"No, it's fine, Leah," the woman replies, in a tone that demands my full attention. "You have the information about our center. We can also help you get set up at some training courses here in the city. What would you like?"

"I like photography." I can imagine the shocked look on their faces. How could a blind woman take pictures, they must be wondering. "I'm busy all day, and . . ." I start to tell them I have a new friend, but stop myself just in time. "I'm writing. Antonia helps me an awful lot," I continue. "If I ever need her to stay with me for the day, she's more than happy to."

"We're very pleased to hear it. We ought to remind you again that we can offer you a guide dog, to make life easier."

"The thing is, I'm allergic," I lie.

"A lot of them are hypoallergenic nowadays . . ."

"Up to now I've been able to get around with my stick. Sometimes I don't even need it."

"Yes, so we can see," replies Julia, taking out some pamphlets and leaving them on the sofa as she stands. "Have a look through these—some of them might be a big help to you."

"I will, of course . . ." I say, hastening to accompany them to the front door.

At that moment, there are two knocks on it. I walk past them and turn before opening it.

"That must be Connor, the building superintendent." It's Alice.

I step aside to let Sharon and Julia leave.

"This is my neighbor," I announce.

When I open my eyes, I see Sharon turned toward Alice. I blink, and the visitors are already down the hall, waiting for the elevator.

I let Alice in and hear her pause at the far end of my front hallway, then tilt her head, as if recognizing the exact spot where we made contact last night. Before going through to the living room, she places her right hand up to the wall, at the same height my hands had been.

She is freshly showered. Her aroma stays in the hallway, just as the image of her with her hand on the wall stays with me. Though I sense she is now looking out at the park, leaning on the glass door.

The living room is filled with the scent of anxiety. Alice has her back to me; her arms are hanging down by her sides.

"Are you okay?" is the only question that comes to mind. I ache for Alice to open up to me, to be able to talk to her about everything that's happened.

Alice turns round slowly and stands in front of me, a blur. I blink and am able to bring her more into focus, like a backlit silhouette.

I step over to her cautiously, but Alice turns her back to me again.

"I can't do this anymore . . ." she murmurs, knowing that I can hear even the softest sigh. "I'm tired of crying."

"We've got to do something," I say, and then immediately correct myself. "You've got to do something. Is it your husband?"

Alice whispers, "Yes," and buries her face in her hands.

"He can't come into your apartment if you don't want him to."

"Leah, he pays the rent."

"That doesn't give him the right—"

"Leah!" she say, interrupting me, as though she can't bear to talk about the man who is torturing her. "He can do whatever he likes."

"So . . ."

"So there's nothing we can do." I'm pleased to hear her say *we*.

"The first thing is to change the locks. I've just had mine done." I move beside her and take her hand. I'm struck by its softness. When I open my eyes, Alice's are closed. I see her face, subtly made up. Underneath her eyes, a purple bruise is mostly hidden with concealer. Her right eye is bloodshot, and there is a small cut on her eyebrow.

"From here it looks as if we don't even live in the city," Alice says, gazing out onto the park. "We live on a hilltop, cut off from all the noise, far away from everyone running to get where they have to be. And the park below, far below, way off in the distance . . . Your place is so full of light," Alice murmurs faintly.

"Yours must be too. Our apartments are laid out the same way," I say. I hug her.

"You could have asked me for help." I reproach her softly yet firmly.

"What could you have done, Leah?"

"Called Connor, the police."

"I'm still his wife. He's a very powerful lawyer; he can do whatever he likes. If he pays for the apartment, he's entitled to a key. You see why I can't get the locks changed? I thought we were going to be okay last night: he told me he wanted to see me to talk about the divorce, that we didn't need to go to court, that way we could avoid unnecessary costs. I believed him. I thought we could do it . . ."

"You can't let him mistreat you."

"When I first met him, he didn't drink. I didn't know he'd previously had an alcohol problem. This last year has been hell. You can't imagine how he gets. No one can control him."

"You can stay with me tonight if you like. There's plenty of room."

"Thanks, Leah, but he's going on a trip today. I don't think he'll be back for a while."

"And what will you do when he comes back?"

"I'm taking each day as it comes. When he returns, we'll just have to see. Maybe I should simply disappear, so that he can't find me, but how do I do that? I'm at the point of just surrendering, letting him do what he wants. I've already accepted the fact that I'll live a short life—"

"You can't let him get away with it, Alice," I say, interrupting her.

"But he will. It doesn't matter how many months or how many years go by. He'll get what he wants."

We leave the apartment a bit disoriented, and at the entrance to the building, we run into Connor. In the daylight, the bruise below Alice's eye is clearly visible. When he sees it, Connor cocks his head.

"Run into something there, Miss Alice?"

She gives him a tight-lipped smile and looks away.

"Women need a good line of defense these days," he says.

"What do you mean? Are you suggesting we buy a gun?" I reply sarcastically. Head bowed, Alice doesn't say a word.

"Not a gun, no, but a can of mace, or a knife maybe. Just something that would scare anyone who comes into your apartment without an invitation."

So he must know about Alice's husband's visits. She must have told him during their heart-to-hearts.

"Just ignore him," Alice says, as we start to walk away, her arm through mine.

"Did you know Connor before you moved here?" I ask.

"Why would you think that?"

"Maybe he can help you." I don't want to let her know that Olivia saw the two of them talking.

Alice seems taken aback. "I met Connor when I moved in. He's a little strange, but has otherwise been very kind, that's all. I've told him that I'm going through a divorce."

"I think we should go for a walk. It'll do you good," I say.

Although a knife's not a bad idea either, I think.

Alice walks by my side with some difficulty, as if the touch of her clothes hurts her, as if her body is covered in bruises.

SEVENTEEN

Springtime is in limbo, awaiting a blizzard or a heat wave.

I glimpse an oblique mass of students with enormous light blue capes and a red trail of light through the middle, as though a car suddenly plowed diagonally through them. An old woman is sheltered from the sun underneath a flowery parasol. In the background, an ambulance siren, a baby crying, and a couple on the corner gossiping in Spanish.

A sign taped up to a lamppost reads: "Sam is missing. He's a ten-year-old shih tzu. He's deaf and blind." I imagine Sam gnawed by rats in the park, returning at some point to his owner, who by then won't want to take him back. Who wants a dog that's deaf *and* blind? At least I have good hearing. And my sense of smell is second to none.

"Can you take the subway?" Alice asks. Her face is lit up, and the bruise is fading on her flushed cheek.

I shrug, a little surprised at the suggestion. I can't remember the last time I took the subway. But I'm not about to admit that, and so decide to go along with her suggestion. My heart begins to race as we take the escalator down.

There are no conversations happening near the turnstiles. Going down to the platform all I can make out is the sound of a violin playing, overlaying a murmur of voices. I am bombarded by the smell of grease, metal, and damp. Alice lets go of my arm for a moment, making me feel disoriented.

When I hear the squeal of an approaching train on the platform below us and the repetitive, electronic voice of the station announcer, I take out my stick and unfold it. It will keep me from stumbling through this unknown, fast-moving environment.

Alice swipes her MetroCard twice, and ushers me to the other side of the turnstile.

"Let's go to the last train car," she says, and I nod.

I notice a motionless mass headed toward me and keep moving with my eyes open, passing figures who step aside when they hear the sound of my stick.

"Oh, I'm sorry . . ." I hear someone say.

"Where are we going?" I shout up to Alice, who is walking in front of me.

"I need to get out of the neighborhood. You'll see."

Once we finally reach the end of the platform, I go over to the white tiled wall and lean against the mosaics that spell out the name of the station: Columbia University. Alice crosses the yellow line near the platform edge. I open my eyes and am alarmed to see her leaning over into the dark, empty space, looking toward the mouth of the tunnel.

"Come over here—the train's coming," I call out.

The only sound I can hear now is the racket of the train clattering along the rails. The vibration shudders through me for several seconds. I walk slowly toward the yellow line, still with the image of Alice on my retinas, her body leaning forward, as though a single puff of air could make her lose her balance and be hit by the train. I go to one of the iron columns where the station numbers are written in black and white and hold on to it with both arms. I close my eyes as tightly as I can as the train flies into the station at full speed.

I take my phone out, and, as I take a photo of Alice, I drop my stick. I hug the column with all my might, as though trying to stop the trail of light traced by the train from tearing me in two, until the final carriage comes to a halt in the station.

The doors open. Alice picks up the stick and holds it out to me with a smile.

"Thanks," I say, still startled. I take my stick and step into the car with its yellow and orange seats. Alice guides me to one; she stands nearby, holding on to a pole.

I spend the entire journey with my eyes closed, not saying a word, conscious only of the noise and a new mixture of smells.

A man passes through selling bottles of water. He is shouting, "Only two dollars!" pushing past anyone who gets in his way.

I'm thirsty but remain silent when Alice shoos him away with her hand.

"Whatever, bitch!" he shouts.

Twenty minutes later, when we get off at 14th Street, I ask Alice to find me a subway map. I want to memorize the different lines and stations.

I let Alice lead me out of the labyrinthine station. We walk southeast for several minutes until we come to a tree-filled space, which appears to be circular.

We sit on one of the benches on the northwest side of Washington Square Park. I fish out my phone and take a photo of the empty bench opposite.

"May I see?"

With a shy smile, I pass Alice my phone. She swipes through my photos intently and pauses to examine several of Morningside Park taken from my window. "You should study photography," she says.

"Thanks, but it's just a hobby, really, things I post online," I say.

"I think it would be good for you. You should check out the International Center of Photography website. They have lots of courses for different levels."

Yes, I should give it a shot. Alice makes me feel like a normal girl; she helps me embrace my independence.

"I need something fun, like your photography. I used to love the theater," she says. "When I went to college I joined a group. But I don't think I was ever a very good actress."

I smile.

"That's where I met Michael," Alice says, and points to a lovely four-story town house with pink bricks, a white door, and white window shutters.

"It was at a party one of the deans threw. I dropped out of school to be with him."

"What did you study?" I ask.

"Psychology. Can you believe it? A bag of nerves like me. I came from Ohio to study in New York. I wanted to get away from my town, my family."

"Where in Ohio are you from?"

"Springfield. I got into NYU, and thanks to a scholarship and a loan I was able to move to New York."

"You should have carried on with your studies." I saw myself in her. I would have liked to have gone to college, but my mother was obsessed with protecting me.

"Yes, I know. It would all have been different. But there's no going back now. I was very young, I was lonely, and this is a tough city. I met him at that party, and within a month I was living with him. It was what I needed at that moment. A man who was charming, se-cure, successful. Then I got pregnant."

"You had a child?" When I ask the question, I lean forward, searching for Alice's face. I want to see the expression in her eyes, the happiness, the pain. But I can't. Alice won't stop moving.

"I stopped going to class and to the theater group. We went on a trip. We traveled all over Europe. I'd never left the States before."

"What happened to your child?"

"When I was five months pregnant, I fainted and fell down a

flight of stairs. It was just as well. He never really wanted children."
Silence, then: "Why don't we go and get something to eat?"

But I want to know everything.

"Why did you marry him after that? You could have left him at
that point."

"I fell into a deep depression, and he helped me through it. A
year later we got married. At his friends' house in the Hamptons. It
was lovely. Things were good until he started drinking again. Every
time he had problems at work he would turn to alcohol. It was his
outlet. But he's not himself when he drinks."

"And your family?"

"I prefer not to talk about them. As far as I'm concerned, I don't
have any family. Family is forced upon us. You're my family now. We
chose each other, right?"

My hand, resting on top of my thigh, is suddenly blanketed by
hers. It feels like a promise.

"Yes, let's eat something," I say happily.

We go into a little café on Seventh Avenue and purchase sand-
wiches and two bottles of water. We walk toward the Hudson. I
keep my eyes closed, and we climb some stairs to sit on the High
Line. I measure each step, calculate the weight of the noises. I dare
not open my eyes.

"Alice, if you don't go to the police, you should at least hire a
lawyer," I say. "You need someone to look after your interests in this
divorce."

"Yeah, I know. I'm thinking of making an appointment this week.
Will you come with me?"

"Of course."

We take a cab back uptown, and I open the window when we get
on the Westside Highway. I imagine the wind sweeping away all of
Alice's worries. When we get out at Amsterdam Avenue and 116th
Street, she gives me a quick hug and kisses me on both cheeks.

"See you on Wednesday," she says. "I have to do some shopping."

"Shall I come with you?"

"No need, but thanks anyway. Take care!" she shouts as she walks away.

When I reach the door of my apartment, there is a long, narrow wooden box sitting on top of the welcome mat. I lean down, pick it up carefully, and, as I give my new key an extra tug and push the door open, I sniff the entrance to make sure nobody has been inside. Going straight to the kitchen, I open the box. With my eyes closed, I feel the edges of the object inside, and the cold chill of metal takes me by surprise: it's a knife.

I pause with my hand on the black polished wooden handle and the silver guard that supports the blade, then gently test the sharp edge with my fingertip. I try to find Connor's scent. I can't. Should I thank Connor for this present? I take the knife to my bedroom and place it in the drawer of my bedside table.

Before going to bed that night, I listen for sounds through the wall. I pause on the wooden floorboards to feel even the slightest vibration, but Alice isn't home.

Throughout the night, each time I am about to drop off to sleep, I open my eyes at the slightest sound. This goes on until dawn.

EIGHTEEN

In New York, the corridors in prewar buildings are dark and gloomy, designed to produce a sense of contrasting grandeur upon entering the vast apartments. On Dr. Allen's floor, the hallway is long and twisted. Whenever I walk past his elderly next-door neighbor's apartment, he opens his door to see who it is. I am convinced he does this with every patient who passes by.

"Do you know your neighbor next door?" I ask the doctor, as I stand by his window.

"He's a hermit; he's been living in the building for years."

"Every time he hears the elevator, he pokes his head out to see who's coming to visit you."

"I know. He once protested because he didn't want me to receive my patients here. Don't pay him any attention."

"I imagine he must be put out seeing all the crazies go by . . ."

"I'm not even going to dignify that with a response, Leah." He waves his hand impatiently. "How are you getting on with your new friend?"

"Alice, her name is Alice."

"Have you been seeing one another?"

"She could almost be a therapist, like you. I think she studied psychology." I hear Dr. Allen's felt-tip pen scratch at his notebook. "But only for a couple of years. . . . She thinks I ought to study photography."

Silence

"I enjoy making images," I explain.

"Leah, you've never been inside a classroom. You were educated at home. Your mother . . ."

"Before I was eight, I used to go to school," I reply defensively.

"Well, let's see . . . a summer course or something similar?"

"Forget it. It's just a project I thought was interesting. I can't make things complicated for myself."

"Leah, I'm not saying you shouldn't do it. Just that—"

"I think I could give it a try. Last night I went to the International Center of Photography's website. Alice recommended it to me."

I'm upset and show it by folding my arms. Not about the classes or Dr. Allen's doubts, but on behalf of my friend.

"Her husband hit her." There, I said it.

The doctor rises quickly to his feet. He's clearly trying to catch my attention, but I remain still, with my back to him, transfixed by the Hudson River.

"How do you know he hit her?"

I say nothing, trying to appear nonchalant. But in fact, I am searching for the exact words to make Dr. Allen understand Alice's situation.

"Did you see him hitting her?" he insists. I nod and turn to face him.

"I heard them. I asked her if she needed help, but she said no, that everything was fine. She didn't want me to get involved because I could get hurt as well."

"Well then, I hope you two have reported him to the police."

"We can't do that."

"But this man sounds dangerous."

"Only when he drinks," I say, repeating Alice's words with conviction.

Dr. Allen is now impatient. He returns to his desk and closes my file. I consider leaving the session then and there. I've said too much, compromised my friend, abused her trust.

"I'm probably being dramatic. Truth is, it wasn't that serious. It was nothing more than an argument that seemed to turn violent."

"Tell me, Leah, was it violent or not?"

I refuse to answer him, and instead gather my things and walk out of his office. I'm mad at myself for my pathetic need to talk, to make my most intimate feelings known. Or maybe that is Dr. Allen's great talent: to make me talk as if I am in a confessional, as if he were hypnotizing me. I know he's checking for signs, signs of the breakdown I had ten years ago. But I refuse to give him any. What if Alice comes to one of my sessions sometime . . . no, that's a ridiculous idea. Alice would never do anything like that, and in the end it might make the doctor even more suspicious. *What if he decides to call the police and report her husband?*

"He'd have the right to do so. I'm his patient, and it's his duty to protect me," I say out loud as I reach Mont Cenis.

I opt for the stairs but first head to the mailboxes. The postal worker must have left the long aluminum bar that runs along the top of all the mailboxes open, or perhaps someone forced it. I push it as hard as I can toward the wall, and hear the catch click shut. I search for my mail key in my bag and open my mailbox.

There are no letters or bills, only a piece of yellowing cardboard. I wonder if it came off a package and has been in here for weeks at the bottom of the narrow box. I take the ocher-colored card out and see a date written in one corner in smudged red ink: 1889. I move my hand quickly, and the card becomes a cloud. Placing it in front of my face, I open my eyelids slowly and can feel my heart skip a beat. I take a deep breath and hold as much air as possible in my lungs until I feel it beating again.

The gilt-edged card has a dark oval in the middle. On it I can make out a white-haired baby girl dressed in lace. I am taken aback by a disturbing detail: the child has no eyes. In their place are holes. I drop the photograph and raise my hands to my nostrils, checking for a hint of bergamot, but all I can detect are traces of dust and a faint odor of wood and ink. On the back, I can barely see handwriting: *We see more than you can imagine.*

I pick the photograph back up and start to walk toward the stairs, certain that someone has tampered with the mailboxes and I am being watched. Halfway to the stairs, I come to a halt, listen intently, and decide instead to take the elevator to the third floor. There is no one else in the lobby, but someone could be hiding between two floors on the staircase. My sense of smell has deserted me.

When I reach the third floor, I run to my apartment and struggle with the key. The first thing I hear is the sound of a trumpet and a piano. Music? Someone is listening to a song in the dining room.

Stealing along the hallway, I recognize "Blue in Green." I enter the room, determined to confront whoever is there, but find it empty. Yet again, someone has been inside my apartment. An image of the bears coming after Goldilocks occurs to me. Connor, it must have been Connor. *Are they trying to drive me crazy?* I order the music in the sound system to switch itself off and make a note to disconnect Alexa—anybody can activate her speakers from a distance.

Leaving the card on the dining room table, I go over to my laptop and open Google. I'm not sure what exactly I'm looking for. First I type in the year, "1889," then "photograph," followed by "children" and the letter "b." I pause for a moment, then complete the word: "blind." The first result takes me to an auction on eBay. Someone is selling daguerreotypes, antique photographs that cost hundreds of dollars.

There are images of families, couples on their wedding day, a woman with a child asleep in her arms. They all appear like ghosts. Their eyes are all blank, staring into space.

I order lunch over the phone and wait patiently for the delivery boy. I want to forget the daguerreotype. I consider getting rid of it or destroying it, but in the end hide it in the bottom drawer of the dining room sideboard. As I close the drawer, my uneasiness returns. Who is trying to scare me? Alice's husband? But why? Because I witnessed his abuse? No, this is a warning. I can't talk to anyone about Alice anymore, about her mistreatment, the divorce. I must stay away from my neighbor from now on, or else my eyes will be gouged out too.

I greet the delivery boy with a timid smile this time. But he's in a hurry; his forehead is sweaty, and the roots of his hair are dark with moisture. He must have other orders to deliver. He doesn't touch my arm as he usually does, that subtle caress I yearn for. He leaves quickly, and I shut the door carefully. Pausing in the hallway, all I can hear from the adjoining apartment is a profound silence. Alice must be either out or napping. Tonight I should try to sleep eight, ten, twelve hours if I can.

Hours later, I secure all the doors and windows and switch on the air-conditioning in my bedroom. I am about to take a shower but change my mind and decide to fill the tub. I wait until it is almost overflowing and submerge myself in the narrow, solid sea. I float with my eyes closed, then doze off for several minutes.

The slamming of my neighbor's door awakens me. I can't tell if Alice has just arrived or is on her way out. Concentrating hard, I hear her enter the elevator. Where could she be going at this time of night? Still wet, I throw on my white bathrobe and look out the French doors, hoping to spot her on the sidewalk. I blink several times but can't locate her, only the occasional passerby. Then behind the guard post, on the steps leading down into the park, I see Alice wearing a scarlet dress. I blink several times to see where she is headed, but she stays rooted to the spot, like one of my stored-up images. It's as if I never blinked.

A man, I can see a man behind the Columbia guard. He appears and disappears. Is he talking to Alice? Alice turns around, and the two are face-to-face, separated. I blink again and I can define that figure a little more. My brain is in league with my eyes, playing tricks on me. Is it Mark from the bookstore? It can't be. Why would he be talking to Alice? The man disappears. Alice is alone.

I close my eyes again and count a few seconds, and when I open them once more, Alice has disappeared.

NINETEEN

"Alice!"

I wake with a start at the sound of my own voice.

Could she have heard me? Or maybe it was all in my head. My throat is dry. I swallow and try to make a sound. My white nightshirt is soaking wet with perspiration.

If Alice's husband placed the daguerreotype in my mailbox, that means he hasn't left town. It also means that both Alice and I are in danger. Or maybe he just wants to scare me into convincing Alice to go back to him.

Whatever the case, I am frightened, and I wish I hadn't told Alice I would go with her to her lawyer's office.

After a quick shower, I knock on her door. No one answers. I persist: one, two, three loud knocks. I empty my mind of terrifying thoughts and try to listen.

Just as I'm about to turn away, the door opens.

"Good morning, Leah. Sorry, I overslept," she says. I blink and see her looking back down her front hallway before shutting the door behind her. "Let's go."

Is someone in her apartment?

Alice takes her lipstick out of her bag and applies it carefully. She pushes her hair behind her ears and smooths down her gray-and-white-striped dress. She is more fidgety than usual this morning.

We ride in the elevator without speaking. I can hear Alice rummaging through her bag again, and sense that she's checking messages on her phone. I hear sounds of typing, then the plunk of the phone back in her bag.

"Is something wrong?" I ask.

Alice's outline is blurred each time she moves. She appears and disappears, so that all I can make out are the stripes on her dress.

"I wanted to confirm the meeting with the lawyer this morning," she tells me. "And wanted to check I've got the documents he asked for."

"You've got time to go back and look for whatever you need."

"The marriage certificate, the prenup agreement . . . I don't think I need anything else."

"You signed a prenuptial agreement?"

"Yes, but I don't care. What I want is to be rid of him," Alice insists. "I mean, to get a divorce. I'm not interested in his money. And that exasperates him even more. If this was just about the separation of assets, he would have let me go long ago."

We stop on the corner of 104th Street and Broadway and Alice checks the time on her phone.

"I think you should wait for me here," she says. "This is something I have to do on my own."

"Are you sure?"

"You can have a coffee while you're waiting," she says, pointing to the entrance of a nearby Starbucks.

I do as I'm told and can hear Alice walking toward her lawyer's office as I go in the opposite direction. I feel the urge to turn back and make sure she doesn't change her mind. She's been acting strange all morning. I should have asked her what she was doing in the park last night. I should have warned her about the danger of going into the park at night.

I order a mocha Frappuccino and sit at one of the tables looking onto 104th Street, so that Alice will see me when she comes out.

I drink in slow sips, measuring the time. An hour goes by. I should have brought a book. I'm about to get out my cell phone when I spot Alice.

She is standing, smiling, happy and confident, in the doorway of the Starbucks. As she makes her way toward me, I smell fresh lavender, as though she's just walked through a blossoming field. I hear her bring a chair over to my table, sit down, and plonk her elbows on the surface.

"I think I'm going to get out of this nightmare," she says.

"Good, you've taken the first step."

"You can't imagine how hard it is to find a lawyer to take on a case like this . . ."

"Alice, this city is full of lawyers desperate for clients."

"But none of them wants to take on a case involving another lawyer. Especially one like Michael. That's the problem. At my husband's law firm, they all protect one another; they have no scruples."

"I understand. So what's the next step?"

"He's going to present the divorce petition to the court," she whispers excitedly.

"In other words, very soon your husband is going to receive your documents."

Alice raises her hands to her face and begins to move them so that her features disappear from my sight. To my eyes, she looks as if she is about to topple over.

"Everything's going to be fine," I say.

"I know," she replies, gently wiping away a tear lodged in her eyelash. She yawns and leans her head back against the windowpane.

"Going out so late in our neighborhood isn't such a good idea," I say.

"It's a quiet area. Besides, I don't go out at night."

"I don't think it's a good idea to cross the park at midnight, Alice."

"I wouldn't have the nerve."

"It's not as dangerous as it used to be, but you could run into a drug addict, a mugger, who knows . . ."

"I understand. I don't think I'd venture into Morningside Park or Central Park at night. If I needed to go somewhere on the east side, I'd take a taxi."

"Then what were you doing last night on the park steps at midnight?" I blurt out.

"Leah, I was asleep in my bed at midnight."

"Alice, I saw you standing there at the top of the steps for several minutes. You were wearing a red dress."

"Red? I don't even own a red dress. It's not a color I'd wear, especially not with Michael stalking about. You must have been mistaken."

I'm sure it was her, but I don't want to make her angry. Who knows why she won't admit it? Maybe she bought some drugs or arranged a secret meeting with her husband that she doesn't want to admit to. Maybe she and Connor—or Mark?—arranged a tryst.

We sit in silence for several minutes, and I am assailed with doubts. I need to rest. Maybe it's true that Alice didn't go to the park, didn't put on a red dress, and it's my own exhausted mind that is creating fantasies.

"Do you know what I'd like to do once all of this is over?" she suddenly says excitedly. "Go on a trip. We ought to travel somewhere far away. Just the two of us, to celebrate."

"The farthest I've ever been is Boston."

"Ah, well, I'm talking about crossing the Atlantic, Leah. Let's go to Europe, to Paris!" I am overwhelmed with happiness. All suspicions are wiped away.

"Why not?" I say. "Let's do it! Let's go to Paris this summer."

TWENTY

Ever since Mom's death or, more accurately, ever since Alice moved in next door, I've had the feeling that my eyes are beginning to see movement again. An unsteady flow, perhaps, but a definite improvement. I am using my white stick less and less. Thanks to Alice, light has come back into my life. I am convinced that the coming summer will be the best of my life.

After my Friday-night supper with Olivia, I recognize Alice's knock at the door. It is no more than two gentle taps.

"I've hired a car" is her greeting.

No doubt about it: presenting her divorce petition has revitalized her.

"Early tomorrow morning we're going to drive out of town and go into the country," she announces. I hear her giggling before she envelops me in a hug.

"Thank you for being my friend," she whispers in my ear, then returns to her own apartment.

Closing the front door, I hear my friend enter number 34 and walk down her entrance hall toward her bedroom. I even hear her collapse onto the bed and let out a lengthy sigh. Yet in my eyes,

Alice is still on the threshold, her smile has vanished, and her eyes are about to dissolve.

By the time Antonia arrives early the next morning, I have already eaten breakfast and tidied up my room. As she's setting her bag down in the kitchen, I come up and embrace her from behind.

"Good morning! We're going *upstate*. A journey out into the country and back. I suppose we'll be back late," I say smugly.

"Do you know something, Leah?" Antonia replies slowly. "It's good to trust others, but trusting too much can cost us dearly."

"Alice is a good woman, Antonia."

"I'm sure she is, but she's going through a divorce."

"Is that a reason to reject her?"

"Listen, Leah, it's not a question of rejecting her. All I mean is that nobody should get between a man and a wife. Look at the way those two are now: each wants the other's head on a plate. But in the blink of an eye they could make peace. That's how it is, believe me."

"Don't worry, all I do is listen to her, accompany her, support her . . ."

"You've already been through enough. Remember what happened to Mrs. Orman." Silence. "And all I want is for you not to suffer. Leah . . . you need to stop."

I exit the apartment. As I close the door behind me, I can hear Antonia calling on her saints, imploring them to protect and guide me, to open the way for me, to keep me from all evil, and to renew the most sacred gift: that of sight. Her prayers always end with that request.

When I open the front door to the building, a red two-seater car is parked outside. The person behind the wheel is waving her arms. I blink several times and am able to make out Alice in the midst of a cloud.

"I thought you hated red," I say as I stroll coolly toward the car, without the help of my stick.

"Ah, but this is burgundy—it's not so intense. And it's just a rental. Are you ready?"

As I climb in and close the car door, I can feel Antonia observing us from the French doors above.

"We're like Thelma and Louise!" Alice shouts, but I don't follow. "Like in the movie. Two female friends who drive off in a convertible and together decide to end it all at the Grand Canyon."

My eyes tightly shut, I let the wind buffet me and dissipate all the sounds that are intermingling and drifting away, coming and going until they lose strength. I must concentrate on what Alice is saying in order to adapt to the invasion of uncontrollable sensations that set my pulse racing. We head for the highway.

"You'll see, we're going to cross the George Washington Bridge."

I open my eyes and can make out multicolored trails of light, with the still waters of the Hudson to my left. I take out a silk scarf and wrap it round my throat. I begin taking snapshots on my cell phone. I feel far from danger, the strange daguerreotype, the smell of bergamot, my confessions to Dr. Allen, my white stick, Antonia's warnings.

As we drive onto the bridge, the car comes to a sudden halt, and I hold on to the glove box. A giant mass of interlaced iron appears in front of me, the cables holding up the structure, the huge river on both sides. For a brief moment, the world is a cathedral of latticed metal. Only sound seems to be moving: the car horns, their engines turning over, the squeal of tires, the runners jogging, the murmur of the river. Alice whispers something about traffic.

The bridge seems endless, as if it is being duplicated in front of my eyes, and each section takes me to another, higher one. When we finally reach the summit, it begins to slope down, extending to infinity. The exit presents myriad possibilities: twisting roads that begin or end at the bridge. I notice Alice hesitate as if this is the first time she's taken this route. Then she swerves to the right, following the signs north.

As we enter the Palisades, with the river and Manhattan to our right, a sense of calm returns, as if we are driving along a road through a wood. Alice is driving too slowly now, and the other drivers overtake her in a rage, zigzagging around her. I can feel the speed of the car vibrate inside my organs, and can see the deep green of the trees as if we are in a cave, its walls sliding past us.

We take Interstate 87 and heavy clouds appear above our heads. Another hour goes by in what feels like a fleeting second, and we turn off the highway looking for side roads. Woodstock is about twenty miles away.

Before driving through the town, we cross some abandoned railroad tracks buried in the asphalt, with weeds sprouting through them. We pull up to a public parking lot close to a small, abandoned cemetery, flanked by a piece of wasteland with a flag at half-mast, several abandoned cars, piles of junk, and a mound of reddish earth. Beyond this is a park with a line of stalls selling garishly colored cotton dresses, handmade jewelry, and rocks with special powers (according to the sign). On one corner, a group of children is selling lemonade.

I want to take in every detail, and I cling to Alice's arm as she drives toward the sound of steady drumbeats. When we enter the park, I feel the intensity of the sun begin to gradually diminish. I look up at the sky and see a cloud, outlined by a golden halo.

"It's as if time stopped here, don't you think?" asks Alice. "It's like we're in the sixties." She guides me past ageless hippies and women in cutoff jeans.

On the way up, Alice explained that she and Michael used to rent a house in Dobbs Ferry and would take drives out to Woodstock on the weekends. The idea was to buy a farm someday, away from the city noise. They never did.

Standing in the middle of the crowd, an old man wearing an enormous velvet cape and covered in necklaces and bracelets is watching me. He has on a battered top hat that covers his bald head, with a few wisps of white hair protruding from it that reach down to his long, dry, yellowing beard. He is leaning on an enormous wooden staff, topped by multicolored feathers tied to the wood with leather strips. He is wearing a belt decorated with bells and looks like a kindly old wizard. A sign hangs from his neck declaring that selfies with him are free. I detect a bad odor coming off him, but that image quickly dissolves. What the man smells of is the choking scent of old age.

"He's always here in the spring," Alice whispers in my ear as we approach. "He must have been a hippie, one of those who came to the concert in sixty-nine and never left."

"I don't charge for photos," he says. I feel his eyes on me.

"We already know that, thanks," says Alice. The sound of the drums fades.

"I once lost my sight, just as you have," he says to me. "You don't see other people, but you can see me, because I don't move."

"Leah," whispers Alice, "I think we should keep moving."

"So, you too?" I ask the old man, eyes wide open, examining the time-blackened furrows that trace maps on his battered face. I see a blue glint in his bloodshot eyes. I can hear his voice, but his lips are buried between his mustache and beard.

"I was your age, more or less," he says, lowering his voice as if he wants me, but not Alice, to hear his story. "I tried all the drugs there were and began to trip with the most powerful of all of them. It was like I'd found paradise. One day I woke up and the world came to a standstill, like it has for you now. I can read the silence in your eyes."

"And since then you haven't been able to see the movement?" I ask.

"That's why I stayed here. Far away from everybody—my family, my friends."

"But later you got your sight back?"

"Yes, but don't get your hopes up. The world isn't the way you imagine it to be. One day I woke up and everything around me spiraled away, as if gravity had swallowed it up. I wasn't ready, I wasn't expecting it, and it made me desperate. What have I gained by recovering movement? I feel giddy all the time. The world spins round me too quickly."

I feel Alice take me gently by the arm and guide me out to the street, not giving me time to say goodbye to the man. But his image persists in my eyes.

"He's crazy, don't listen to him," Alice says, but I am shaken.

I've never met anyone else like me before.

Out in the esplanade, I am hit by a mixture of smells. I hear hundreds of people gathered in the open space. I begin to tremble at the dust and the sounds of shoulders bumping into shoulders. I let myself be carried along by the crowd.

"When spring comes, they hold this antique fair every Saturday," Alice explains enthusiastically. I can't make her out properly in all the surrounding chaos. "Lots of people come from the city just to buy old furniture."

Then she grabs me by the arm and steers me to one of the stalls.

"Don't move!" she hisses.

Opening my eyes, I catch sight of Alice's panicked face. I look down, blink, and in the stall see hundreds of daguerreotypes, some of them framed. The eyes all seem to have been gouged out. In all of them, I see my mother and father and me, at age eight.

"Leah!" Alice insists, demanding my full attention. "He's here!"

Suddenly I understand. I flare my nostrils and begin to sniff. I search anxiously for the smell of bergamot but can't find it.

"Are you sure?"

"Leah, I saw him in profile, behind me," Alice says. I blink and try to spot him.

"Don't move!"

Everything I make out is in fragments. A woman carrying a baby with no legs. A white-haired man's head floating in streaks of light. A man dressed in black without a head. Could that be him? I'm blinking constantly to refresh the images, but everything is such a jumble. I concentrate on the bergamot smell, ignoring the stallholders' insistent cries, the shouts of the passersby, the drumbeats. The only smells I can detect are those of confusion and fear.

"Let's go," I hear myself say. I take Alice by the arm and drag her away in the opposite direction.

I hear Alice's ragged breathing, then her coughing and swallowing hard. Her hands are cold and sweaty. I can't see her face but imagine her eyes brimming with tears.

"I think we've given him the slip," she says, seemingly calmer.

"Let's go back to the city," I order.

"No!" she exclaims. "I won't allow Michael to ruin our Saturday. It's our day, not his. Let's find somewhere to have lunch."

We go to an Asian restaurant, where only a couple of tables are taken. We sit side by side in a corner, guarding the entrance.

I let Alice order for me and sip at my glass of water nervously.

"I thought your husband was away on a trip," I say, clearing my throat.

"He must have come back." Alice seems more resigned than anxious.

"Are you sure it was him?"

Alice raises her glass to her lips but doesn't take a drink. "I don't know. . . . This water is too cold," she says, and signals to the waitress. "Can you bring me a glass of water with no ice?"

"Maybe you got it wrong," I say.

"Maybe."

"There were too many people at the fair . . ."

"Yes, there were too many," Alice says soothingly. "I'm sorry if it was too much for you."

"Who else knew you were coming to Woodstock? Did you tell anybody? The only person I told was Antonia."

"Nobody else knew. I don't tell anyone about myself. Only you."

"So how could he know we were coming to Woodstock? It's two hours from the city."

"I rented the car last night at an agency. I was going to pay cash, but they required a credit card. My credit card is linked to his." Alice swallows hard. "I guess he figured I would come here."

We eat our lunch without speaking. I feel Alice's hands tremble each time she drinks a spoonful of her miso soup. I don't ask any more questions. Each time a new customer walks in, we both look up.

"I'm going to the bathroom," I hear Alice say in a thick, weary voice.

I am convinced Alice made a mistake. At no point did I perceive any trace of Michael's smell or sense his energy. Yes, Alice must have been mistaken.

As I consider all the possibilities, I lose track of the time. Almost a quarter of an hour goes by, and Alice hasn't come back to the table.

"Are you all right? Do you need anything?" asks the waitress.

"The bathroom . . . could you show me where it is?"

"Of course. I'll go with you."

"There's no need. You just have to tell me where it is."

"Are you sure?"

I nod impatiently.

"It's on the right at the end of the corridor."

The main room in the restaurant is painted a bright orange, almost yellow. I walk down the corridor, and as I turn right, a flash of light from the service door blinds me.

I run toward it and sniff the air, but all I can detect is the stench of kerosene and rotten vegetables from the garbage.

"Alice!" I shout, to no effect.

To my right, I see that the bathroom door is ajar. I walk slowly toward it, counting every one of my heartbeats.

I fill my lungs with thick air and gather enough strength to open the bathroom door. I go in, eyes closed. Apart from the smell of detergent, I can hear the faucet running.

Opening my eyes, I find Alice curled up in a corner.

"Oh my God!" cries the waitress, who is suddenly behind me.

"It's nothing." Alice's quavering voice floats through the confined space. "I feel better now."

Even after we walk back to the table, my retinas hold the image of Alice, head between her knees, curled up into a ball.

"The check please," I hear her say, her voice steady once more. "Leah, it's time to go."

On our way to the parking lot, Alice begins to cry. "How long is this going to continue?" she whimpers. "He came into the bathroom, but I was too scared to tell you."

"Did he hurt you? Did he say anything?"

"Just seeing him hurts me. It makes my stomach churn. I feel like throwing up."

"I think it's time for you to report him."

"He must have followed us, and then he came in through the back door of the restaurant. He told me he was going to fight it, that it's not going to be easy for me to get rid of him. He's been drinking. How can he drive in that state? He left when he heard you coming down the hall."

"At least he didn't hurt you. Calm down, this nightmare will soon be over. Are you up to driving?"

"Yes, don't worry, it will do me good."

We head back toward the city without a word. I want to ask more questions, now that Alice seems calmer. Leaving behind the bends and inclines of the country roads, we merge onto Interstate 87.

The traffic is light. Every now and then trailers go by at twice our speed, making the small red convertible shake. As we leave Ulster County behind, I can tell Alice's breathing has changed. She lets out a piercing scream and angrily presses down on the accelerator. She begins to weave in and out, overtaking the cars in front of us.

I blink and see Alice glance in the rearview mirror, then to the side mirrors, as she speeds past anyone who gets in her way.

"He's following us! He's going to make us crash!"

I keep my eyes closed and try to find the words to calm her.

"If you'll just slow down—"

"Leah, he's following us!" Alice shouts.

"We're going to have an accident."

"That's what he wants!"

Alice beeps her horn incessantly at a white truck, which moves over to let her pass. Now there is no one in front of us, and Alice presses the accelerator to the floor.

The car begins to bounce. I can feel it slide to one side, until it comes to a sudden stop. I cling to my seat belt, and Alice throws out her arm as if to protect me. Then I hear a dull thud against the front windshield, and the car engine dies.

When I open my eyes, I see we are enveloped in a cloud of dust, tilted over in the right-hand roadside ditch.

"Are you hurt?" Alice is leaning over me, examining my face, pushing back my hair.

"I'm fine, fine. What about you?"

Cars begin to move slowly past. Some of them check that we are all right and continue on their way. No one stops to help.

"I'm so sorry, Leah."

"I think we should carry on, but carefully, Alice . . ."

Alice takes a deep breath and puts the car into gear, but it doesn't move. I lower the sun shield and look into the small passenger mirror. Noticing flecks of blood on my lips, I close my eyes and begin to wipe it away. I feel a sudden pain in my stomach.

"Leah, you're bleeding!" Alice shouts in panic, unbuckling her seat belt.

"I must have bit myself. I don't think I banged into anything."

With a sigh, Alice buckles up her seat belt again and accelerates cautiously. The car begins to move until, tugging violently at the wheel, she manages to steer it out of the ditch and back onto the highway. She stays in the right lane and remains within the speed limit the rest of the way.

We reach Morningside Drive before nightfall. We come to a stop in front of the Boston ivy that is spreading rapaciously over Mont Cenis's redbrick facade. For an instant, the ivy makes us feel protected. That night, Alice sleeps in my bed beside me.

TWENTY-ONE

"You see what you are thinking. Your eyes are simply the filter of your thoughts, your ideas." Mom's voice echoes in my mind as I slowly emerge from a deep sleep.

By the time I get out of bed, Alice has already left. In the kitchen, Antonia holds out a piece of paper with a weary gesture: *I'm catching the nine o'clock train to Philadelphia to visit my cousin. I'll see you in a couple of days*, Alice has written. She has big, loopy handwriting.

"Spend time with her." Antonia waves her arms in the air. "But don't get involved in her life," she says, emphasizing each word. "If your mother were alive . . ."

"But she isn't, Antonia. I will be fine. Alice will be fine: her nightmare is almost over."

I am trying to convince myself as much as Antonia, but something about Alice's note is nagging at me.

"Have your coffee." Antonia raises her arms to the heavens, throws back her head, and starts muttering to her deities.

She shouldn't even be here. It's Sunday. But I don't ask questions as Antonia begins taking everything off the kitchen shelves—plates, cups, dishes—and wiping everything down.

I go over to the dining room table and spread out the subway map. I am determined to explore the city from one end to the other, to get to know all its hidden nooks and crannies, the way I used to explore the park with Dad. I'm content, studying the colors of the subway lines—green, red, orange, blue, and yellow—when I feel Antonia standing behind me, looking over my shoulder.

"I think it's time you moved. Too many deaths weigh on these walls."

"Antonia, this building dates from 1905, of course lots of people have died here. Besides, this is my home. I like it here." I'm tempted to add that if she doesn't, she needn't come back. But I don't say that.

"What this apartment needs is a good clean. There are too many bad vibes! If you went around barefoot, you'd feel it. Look at the goose bumps it gives me just thinking about it!"

Antonia places her hands firmly on my shoulders.

"Leah, you are like a daughter to me . . ."

"I know, Antonia. But everything is going to be all right."

"Your mother is to blame, because after the accident . . ." She pauses, knowing she is entering forbidden territory. "If it had been me, I would have put the apartment up for sale and moved you far away from the city. Somewhere surrounded by nature, far from noise and other people and the past. But no, she insisted it was here that you could get around without problems, even with your eyes shut."

"People can't just up and move whenever they want to, whenever there's a mishap. Mom grew up here, and so did I."

"Leah, a change always does one good. Bad energy attracts the worst—"

I know Antonia means well, but I can't listen to another word from her. I've heard all of this before. I fold the map, give Antonia a quick kiss goodbye, and head for the front door. As I close the door behind me, I remember that Alice told me she doesn't have any family. So why did she write that she was visiting her cousin in Philadelphia?

TWENTY-TWO

That night I turn the air conditioner off and spread an additional blanket over my comforter. My throat is sore, my forehead is clammy, and my nose is stuffed up. I have a cold.

I need water but would rather stay in bed. The apartment is completely dark. I pick up my cell phone off the bedside table and text Alice:

When are you back? I hope everything's going well and you're getting some rest.

I don't hit send. If she writes to me, I will reply.

I put the phone back down and stare up at the ceiling. Perhaps Antonia is right. I need to get out of this apartment.

In the darkness, shadows parade in front of me. I conjure the images of Mont Cenis's former residents. According to building legend, the original owner of apartment 33 was a rich, middle-aged bachelor. He purchased the apartment hoping a wife and family would follow, but he died before that ever happened. I picture the man's anguished face and imagine him walking past the chandelier in the dining room, its crystal teardrops tinkling, and out through the French doors into the void.

Number 33 remained empty for years until it was sold to my

grandparents after World War II. They had already lived here for twenty years when Mom was born. Its quiet location near two parks made their transition to parenthood easier. I imagine them cuddled on the living room sofa, marveling at the baby girl who came to them so unexpectedly in middle age.

After their deaths, my mother inherited the apartment and a huge bank account. Years later, it was she cuddling on the sofa with my father, marveling over me. "We'll always see the sunrise from here," my parents often repeated. We were lucky to have such an amazing view.

But soon the happy images dissolve, and I am awakened by the smell of bergamot.

Like a scorching breeze, it covers me. I feel my body being pushed facedown onto the mattress. I can't breathe.

The sound of the intruder's movements tells me he is tall and thin. But he is strong. He is not breathing heavily, nor is he perspiring. I sense the bergamot essence is concentrated on his skull, and then imagine it spreading all over his body, then making its way to mine. I'm scared yet ecstatic, repulsed. I begin to tremble.

I cry out weakly and feel a tear at my throat. Why is he here? What is he looking for? Does he think Alice is here?

I remember the knife in my bedside drawer, but I am paralyzed. I could call him by his name, say to him, *Michael, it's finished. There's no going back. You have to let her go.*

I raise my head slightly from the bed, searching for breath, and just as I am about to turn my face toward him, I feel a sharp blow that pushes me back down onto the sheets. The stealthy footsteps are weighty now. I feel the strength in every muscle of his arm. He's using his right hand to hold me down, while his left hand squeezes my breast and reaches down to my buttocks. He isn't wearing a ring or a wristwatch. I remain completely still, hold my breath, and when I recover, scream as loudly as I can.

Turning on his heel, the man crashes out of the room. He opens the front door to the apartment, then closes it so violently that the walls shake. My heart is racing as I take in more oxygen. I can feel my throat bleed.

I am awake through the rest of the early hours but remain frozen in bed. When I eventually sit up, the soft light of the morning is at my window. I breathe in through my nose and out my mouth and feel an unusual calm pass over me. My throat is no longer sore. My muscles are not achy. I brush my hair off my face and calculate the distance between me and the nightstand.

Next time I will use the knife.

TWENTY-THREE

I strip the bed and throw my sheets and pillowcases on the floor. Running to the bathroom, I get into the shower, determined to scrub away every last hint of bergamot. I cover myself in foam and wash my hair so as to get rid of any trace of the intruder. I'm frustrated that I wasn't able to get a good look at him. Then I realize I never will. He must know about my condition, that the slightest movement will guarantee him complete protection.

I dress and make myself a coffee from the Nespresso and stare out the glass doors. I consider telling someone about the incident, but if so, who? Connor? Alice? The police? But then what would Dr. Allen say when he found out? And the social workers? I would argue it was my neighbor's problem, harassment by an alcoholic husband. None of this has anything to do with my lack of sight or my ability to live on my own. It's Alice who should be looked after and sent somewhere safe, not me.

I decide I need answers more than safety right now.

I take the daguerreotype out of the dining room sideboard and grab my handbag. I reach Book Culture faster than usual, ignoring the car honks and the insults along the way.

Mark is at his post behind the cash register when I walk in. As usual, I do my best to cut off all my senses so I won't be overwhelmed by my surroundings.

"Hey, Leah, it's great to see you!"

"Thanks, Mark." I rest my hand at a front table to catch my breath. Mark pulls away and lowers his head as if running away from me.

"It's been a while. . . . I thought you must have changed bookstores." I imagine him smiling.

"I wouldn't know where else to go," I quip.

"Maybe you got stuck on the other side of the looking glass," Mark says, and chuckles.

"That's me. Just like Alice."

The shop is deserted. With my eyes closed, I step closer to the front counter, carefully pull the daguerreotype out of my purse, and show it to him.

"Have you ever seen anything like this?"

"Wow, a daguerreotype." His eyes light up when he sees *1889* marked on it.

Mark mumbles the cryptic dedication—*We see more than you can imagine*.

"Cool. Are you wanting to sell it? I know of a collector upstate. He might be interested," he offers. "By the way, the woman you left with the other day came back and bought several books about blindness."

Alice. She's the one I should be talking to about all this. Should I call her? Text? I hear Mark typing on his phone.

"Thanks, Mark." I wish I could stay and talk. It's been a long time since I've had his full attention like this. *Don't go, stay with me*—his voice in my head is full of yearning.

"Leah." From behind me, I hear his voice, deep, as if in a whisper. If only he came closer, if he came to me and hugged me. No, Mark wouldn't dare. I'm the one who has created a distance with my cane.

"I'll be here at the same time tomorrow," I tell him, and he remains silent. Does he smile? Is he waving goodbye with his hand?

"See you tomorrow," he says, and I pull myself away and exit the store. Using my stick this time, I reach Amsterdam Avenue. I sense someone is following me. I speed up and can feel someone walking in long strides to catch up with me. I stop at the corner, wait for the light to change, and before crossing, I turn around. Mark? No one is there. I'm alone. I cross the street and walk the rest of the way home.

I blink and spot Alice and Antonia at the corner of 116th Street. I blink again, and Alice is standing alone in front of Mont Cenis.

"Alice!" I shout, and she rushes over to me.

I don't wait for a hello, for news about her trip, or for her to tell me why she stayed away only one night. I blurt out: "Michael broke into my apartment last night. I know it was him. I think it's time we go to the police."

"Oh God, Leah, I'm so sorry," she replies. "I'm so sorry I got you caught up in this mess. The only reason he would have broken into your apartment would be to get to me. The only thing to do now, to keep you safe, is for me to move, disappear from New York. I have no alternative."

"But what about your divorce!"

"Listen to me, Leah, you can't imagine what he is capable of."

Our voices begin to overlap, and my static image of Alice blurs. Nothing seems right. I feel like the bergamot has done something to me, increased my blindness.

Alice takes both of my hands in hers and faces me.

"Leah, you need to stay away from me: you can see I'm harming you. My husband destroys everyone and everything that is close to me. You don't know him."

"Please, Alice . . ." *I'm here to help you, you are my only friend,* I want to say. But instead I ask: "What did Antonia want?"

"Antonia?"

"Yes, my housekeeper."

"Oh, nothing. She bumped into me on the street corner. I think she just apologized, but I couldn't really understand her. I was lost in my own thoughts."

We enter the building in silence. Alice hastens her pace, as if she wants to run away from me. When we reach our apartments, Alice turns to me. I blink constantly, my only way to understand her, to know what's going on. Alice squeezes my elbow firmly and says: "Seriously, though. I think it's best if we stay away from one another. I'm going inside now. I have plans to make."

Alice steps into her apartment, her door closes with a resounding thud, and I'm left there in a state of panic. I should have insisted, begged her not to do anything foolish. I forgot to show her the daguerreotype.

My apartment is devoid of odor. Antonia must have scrubbed away the bergamot perfume with her disinfectants in the short time I was out. Even so, the scent is imprinted on my memory. I go to my bedroom and find my bed made with clean sheets. The soiled ones have been placed in the laundry bin. On my pillow, I find a little St. Lucy card. On the back she has written: *Oh, St. Lucy, true LIGHT of holiness, purest virgin and martyr, I, your unworthy devotee, on my knees before you, beg you for the grace to preserve the sight of my dear Leah's eyes so as to put them in the service of the hand of GOD, and to the benefit of her soul and that of her neighbor. So be it. Amen.*

I clutch it to my chest. I appreciate Antonia's good intentions, but her prayers will do nothing to ward off the intruder or help my friend.

I think back to my conversation with Alice. I run to my front hallway and listen but can't hear anything coming from Alice's apartment. Could she have left already? I step out onto the balcony and see her standing on the street corner. She is wearing the red dress again, the one she said she didn't own.

I pick up my handbag, unfold my stick, and move quickly down the stairs, afraid Alice has disappeared. But she is still on the corner when I get outside, looking away from me. Then, only a few yards away, I hear footsteps. Alice is walking away from me.

"Alice!" I call out. But she doesn't stop. I follow her to the subway and down to the platform for the uptown train, which has just pulled into the station.

We both step into the front car full of people. Alice takes the first door; I take the second. Between us is a crowd of shadows, but when I fix my gaze on Alice, I see signs of a profound sadness. One, two, three stations go by, until I gradually lose count. Three stations before entering the Bronx, Alice steps off. I follow her through the tunnel of the station; voices, words in Spanish, echo throughout.

I start to feel dizzy, bump into someone, and decide to follow my friend's scent with my eyes closed. By the time we reach ground level, the sun has set. Music coming from stores, shouts of street vendors, and conversations happening on the sidewalk mingle together to form a single aggressive and chaotic sound.

I'm certain Alice knows I'm following her. How could she not? I cross streets trusting she is obeying traffic signals. We traverse an avenue and go up an incline, then down an alleyway. Blaring ambulance sirens stand out above the hubbub of noise. After reaching an open space, Alice heads for a narrow passageway. The city traffic is audible to our right.

We are now on a bridge. Gusts of wind pick up. Bewildered, I open my eyes and see the red dress, duller now that the sun has gone down. Alice's body is a blur; all I can make out is the material of her dress. Around her are stationary runners in T-shirts and shorts, a woman in midair, a pack of dogs that multiplies and dissolves into a tangled brown mass. On one side is an endless trail of light, colored lines that stretch into the distance, for the most part red, yellow, and orange. I think I'm going to faint.

I hold on to the handrail. Beneath me, the raging waters of the Hudson look like solid rock. I crash into one of the bridge's pillars.

As I look up, the cables are suddenly illuminated, as though the impact switched them on. The light stays high up on the towers of the bridge, leaving us in growing darkness.

I begin to lose sight of the red dress. I need to recalculate the distance, to work out how many yards I am from Alice. I take a few steps forward, and the red of her dress becomes more intense: it goes from dark gray to crimson, and finally to scarlet.

I blink again to see exactly where Alice is. I can't lose her again. I close my eyes and inhale deeply, trying to interpret the smells invading my nostrils. But the only smell I can identify is that of defeat. Poor Alice . . .

First image: Alice leaning on the bridge handrail, with the wind whipping her hair. Unable to move, I begin to tremble. In darkness, I imagine the second and third images: Alice jumping headlong but slowly, as if she weighs nothing. Then Alice on the rocky surface that has now turned to water, swallowing her whole. The merciless currents of the Hudson sweeping her body toward the Atlantic.

If I open my eyes, it will be our farewell. But I don't want to open them. I prefer keeping the image of my friend on the bridge in her red dress, not in the depths of the river. Still, I run blindly to where Alice must be. I will do anything to help her, to give her what she wants. Breathless, I take the final step, clinging to the handrail, and when I reach out with my stick, it bumps against an inert body. Opening my eyes, I see the red dress. In it, Alice's body lies in a heap; it appears she's passed out. I kneel down toward her . . . but I drop the stick. It rolls and falls into the Hudson. Reflexively, I go after it, but Alice extends a hand and steadies me. At this point, I'm unsure who is saving who.

"What are we doing here?" she asks me, her voice weary.

I smile and begin to cry. Surprised, I reach over and hug her.

"Are you all right? Do you need help?" It's the voice of a jogger running in place nearby. "Do you want me to call 911?" the man offers.

"Oh, no. We're fine. We'll be going home now," I say, helping Alice up. "I thought I lost you," I say to her.

"I don't know how I got here."

"Neither do I. I just followed you."

We leave the bridge and cross back over the avenue.

"Come on, let me find a taxi," she says. "Close your eyes if you like. You could have hurt yourself: there's so much traffic."

"Me? What about you? It sounds like this was a case of the blind leading the blind," I say, interrupting her.

Alice lets out a quiet laugh. "I guess you're right."

When the cab arrives at Mont Cenis, we run into Connor at the entrance. He drops his cigarette and stubs it out; I can tell he's uncomfortable, as if he's been caught in the act, though from what I can tell it's the same act he does every night. I stop to ask him to install a lock that can only be locked and unlocked from inside my apartment, and he agrees to take care of it.

When we reach the third floor, I extend my hand toward Alice and grip her shoulder firmly.

"You ought to stay with me."

"You know I can't do that. Not after what happened to you last night. If he comes back here, I need to be home so that he doesn't come after you."

"But that means he'll be coming after you."

"Yes, I guess it does."

TWENTY-FOUR

I begin by closing the blinds, and then draw the curtains. I want Dr. Allen's consulting room to be as dark as possible; even the slightest shadow could distract me.

"You haven't had any rest for days . . . I can tell."

I nod and pace anxiously in the silent darkness of the room, caressing the damask of the chair backs.

"We have to find a solution. You can't go on like this: you're doing yourself harm."

I take a seat opposite the doctor and drape my arms exhaustedly over the edge of the chair.

"Can you finish telling me what's wrong? It's been ten years since I last saw you in such a state."

Ten years. When Mom hospitalized me. Something she had sworn she'd never do no matter what. I swallow hard.

"Alice tried to commit suicide."

"She tried to?"

It confuses me whenever he responds with a question.

"She intended to do so," I explain.

"How do you know? Did she tell you?" He sounds nervous.

I'm a little edgy too: I flex the fingers on my right hand. I stand and walk over to the window and consider pulling back the curtains, but then return to the chair.

"I saw her."

Dr. Allen folds his arms; he's waiting for the details.

"She was like a ghost, or a sleepwalker. She left the building, and I followed her."

"That could have been dangerous."

"I couldn't abandon her."

"But you could have asked for help."

"How was I to know that what she wanted to do was throw herself off a bridge?"

"Leah! We have to find a solution to all this. I don't understand why now, just when you were beginning to show that you can be independent, you've ended up getting involved in a virtual stranger's problems."

"Alice needs help."

"I know, but so do you."

I go over to a small antique mirror that hangs over a shelf piled high with files. The mirror is stained. I see my fragmented face: my forehead split in two, one eye covered by a shadow, my mouth a grimace. This is me, this is how I look. I must change the image I'm projecting for Dr. Allen.

"I'll be able to sleep soon," I say, returning to my seat. I'm smiling now, and my brow is perfectly even. "Alice has decided to leave New York. It's what's best for her."

"What about you?"

I can't concentrate on what he is saying: I've got a strange feeling. There are no smells, noises, or lights of significance, and yet I feel a curious weight pressing down on me. It starts at my forehead, then slips down to my throat, and from there to my chest and stomach. As it's about to take hold of my legs, I feel an overwhelming urge to flee. I dash out of the consulting room without saying goodbye. I cross Broadway breathlessly, then the university campus, and stop at the pedestrian crossing on Amsterdam to wait for the green light.

"Everything will be fine," I tell myself.

The walk back to my apartment is endless. I take another deep breath.

Avoiding the elevator, I slowly begin to count the steps one by one, trying to take my mind off things. I should go down to the basement to ask Connor when he is going to install the internal lock. I hear voices coming from the interior courtyard. When I reach the third floor, I pause at the window covered by Mrs. Bemer's stubborn plants. I see the outline of Mrs. Orman still imprinted on the copper roof over the patio, and a chill runs down my spine.

I stop at number 34 and knock gently on the door. No reply. So I knock again, louder this time. Trying to stay calm, I open the door to my own apartment. I press against the hallway wall to see if I can hear Alice, send her a consoling message. Dropping my bag on the floor, I walk toward the living room to see if I might spot her from the French doors.

Maybe she's gone down to the park.

Reaching the end of my hallway, I can make out a hand resting on the carpet in the living room. I approach cautiously. Is it Alice? Did she escape here, and he followed her and attacked her?

I come closer, eyes closed, and when I open them again, I let out a loud cry:

"Antonia!"

She is lying on her back, with her right hand folded across her chest. Sobbing, I feel her face and can tell she is having difficulty breathing.

Antonia responds with a weak wave of her hand but isn't strong enough to do anything more. I rush to my phone and call 911, and then Antonia's husband, Alejo.

"Don't worry, just rest, the paramedics will be here soon. I called Alejo. Don't talk, don't make any effort," I tell her.

Now we are in a hospital room. Antonia had a heart attack. The journey in the ambulance took only a couple of minutes; the hospital is just around the corner from Mont Cenis. The woman who has looked after me for as long as I can remember is lying here, unconscious, hooked up to all kinds of machines. It's a disorienting sight. I fall asleep in a chair next to her bed.

When I wake up, Alejo is standing in the doorway with a bottle of water. Last time I saw him, he was a mountain of a man. Now he is bent and has bushy eyebrows, and the corners of his mouth are struggling with the gravity of the situation.

"It's time for you to go home," Alejo tells me gently. "Thanks for looking after my old lady."

I can hear Antonia breathing, as well as the sound of the monitors registering her heartbeats and the drip of thick liquid in the IV.

With Alejo's image still in my eyes, it seems that everyone around me is aging, growing smaller, drying out. I take hold of Antonia's warm hand. Bending toward her, I see that she is awake and smiling: her eyes are tired, but she looks content, comfortable. I am unable to hold back tears, and I embrace her carefully. I don't want to hurt her. I sob into her neck.

"Antonia, you're all I have left . . . you can't leave me."

I can hear Antonia's steady, powerful heartbeat. She is alive. That's all I need.

"You really gave us a fright, sweetheart," I hear Alejo whisper in his wife's ear.

"You'll have Antonia around for a while yet," she says, lifting her head, but taking care not to disturb any of the cables connected to her.

But then I can sense her convulsing, clearly in pain. My poor Antonia . . .

"Would you like me to call the nurse?" I ask. The image of a smiling Antonia still fills my eyes.

"My child, the pain will always be there—it never grows tired." Antonia's voice comes and goes with her heartbeats. "Once you've become acquainted with it, the pain never leaves you."

I stay by her side day and night for an entire week, going home only for showers and a change of clothes. I make it a habit to avoid the sighs and sobs of the other patients and their visitors. I need peace, not their sadness. I want all my energy focused on Antonia, the person I love the most.

When Antonia is discharged from the hospital, I convince Alejo that she should recuperate at home with me. After all, the hospital is close by if another emergency happens; Antonia can even walk there if she feels ill or needs to go in for a checkup. Even though the doctors say the heart attack has caused no lasting damage, she is still fragile. She needs to rest, to get her strength back, and most importantly, to have someone look after her, even if that someone can't see her when she's moving.

When I'm working as Antonia's caretaker, the voices of my neighbors disappear completely, and the smells grow faint. I hear nothing from Alice. Number 34 is quiet. Maybe she left the city after all. Maybe she's gone back home to Springfield.

My sleep improves. I'm getting nine hours a night, and I'm able to focus on my story writing more than ever. I'm even beginning to build a small following from my Instagram posts.

Emboldened one evening, when the delivery boy appears at the door smelling of sunshine and crowds, I invite him in.

"My name is Pete," he says.

The portrait I formed of him now has a name. He will no longer simply be the "delivery boy," whose smile lulls me to sleep every night.

We have tea and cookies in the dining room. Antonia is on the sofa behind us, knitting a scarf.

I can tell Antonia is eavesdropping, pleased that her little girl is venturing on this strange first meeting, but at the same time protecting her from a boy she hardly knows.

"So you study journalism . . ." I say, realizing for the first time that I must be his elder by at least six or seven years. This I am not used to.

"I finish in two weeks, then I'm off to DC," he says proudly. "I've got an internship."

"Wow. So after all this time, you finally introduced yourself to me, and now you're leaving?" I laugh to cover up my irritation. I feel Pete shrink away.

"I want to study photography," I blurt out.

"Oh yeah, sure, that would be great," he says. He thinks I'm joking.

"What I can't see is movement," I explain nervously, though I'm grateful to have recovered the conversation. "Right now, for example, I can make out your face but not your arms, because you're always moving them around."

Pete guffaws and takes a sip of his tea. I hear his phone hit the table. He's checking it.

"Aw, I'm sorry, but I have to head back to work."

"Oh, no problem. I'll walk you to the door," I reply, and feel Antonia's gaze on me.

In the doorway, Pete stops in front of me and gives me an awkward hug, his long arms loose around my shoulders.

"I'll see you around, Leah."

I listen to him step into the elevator, though on my retinas he is still beside me, giving me that hug, but this time he takes my whole body into his arms and squeezes me tight, not wanting to say goodbye. Then I hear Antonia calling, and I run anxiously to her. I find her standing calmly in the kitchen.

"Leave them. I'll handle it," I say, referring to the teacups and plates.

"You're making me feel useless."

"I just want you to rest. And then tomorrow, I think you should take me to the garden at St. John the Divine, like when I was a little girl."

"Leah, who is going to take who? You can go on your own now."

"But with you it'll be different."

"So you'll be taking me."

TWENTY-FIVE

On the Friday that Antonia leaves Mont Cenis, the voices in the building return.

As I'm carrying her heavy bag to the taxi, I get an image of two men observing me from across the avenue but push them to the back of my mind. I must concentrate on Antonia now. I'm worried that frail Alejo won't be able to properly care for her. More likely, she will be looking after him when she gets home.

"Alejo needs me," she says resignedly. "The old man misses me."

Opening the taxi door, I help her climb inside, slowly.

When I lean in to give her a goodbye kiss, Antonia whispers in my ear:

"Your neighbor is back. She's watching us from her balcony."

If in all these days the husband hasn't appeared, and we haven't heard her calling for help or sobbing, that must mean the divorce has gone through.

I hear the taxi meter start up.

I'm on the verge of begging Antonia not to go, but I don't. I now see what she has seen all along, that Alice isn't good for me, that I can't help her anymore, that getting caught up in her life again will only do me harm.

As the taxi leaves, a strange silence falls on me; it fills the streets, even the oak trees on the sidewalks. It's a dense, troubling lack of sound, which I now must force my way through to get over the threshold of Mont Cenis. I shield myself with the image of Antonia's lovely face, her protective gaze.

Opening the front door releases a rush of voices:

They're going to change the windows in the building. I bet they make us pay for them.

If they carry on with the repairs to number 22, we'll have to move. The ceiling's going to come down on us.

Ouch, that hurts! Let go of me.

Leaving the elevator on the third floor, I can feel Alice hiding behind her door, peering through the peephole.

As I approach my apartment, I notice a small crack in the wall between numbers 33 and 34. I hear Alice turn the lock. The door opens slowly, and the light from the corridor reveals a shoulder, then Alice's arm, her hands. Her face is not yet visible.

"It's all over," she says.

I put my key in the lock, turn it as hard as I can, and smile. "That's wonderful. It's about time. You see? There's a solution to everything."

"Leah . . ."

With my hand still on my key, I turn. My smile is so wide it hurts.

"So your divorce has gone through?" I ask.

"He has all the documents and has accepted them. He's going to bring them to me, signed, in a few days. He understands that there's no going back, that we each have to get on with our lives, apart from one another."

"I'm happy for you."

"There's no reason to worry, Leah," Alice continues. "I'm sorry for getting you involved in this . . . really, truly sorry."

"It wasn't your fault. What else could you do? The good thing is that he's finally going to leave us . . . I mean," I stammer, "that he's finally going to leave *you* in peace."

"My lawyer says he looked quite calm, that he didn't seem upset."

I want to say: *Don't trust him. You're very naive, and you know what he's like when he drinks. I'm sure that when he spoke to the lawyer he didn't have a drop of alcohol in his system.* But instead I say: "That's good news. I'm happy for you."

"We ought to go on a trip," Alice says, interrupting my thoughts.

"Back to Woodstock?"

"No, Leah, to Paris. We really must go there this summer! I owe you that. By then this nightmare will be over. Once the documents are signed, he'll have to leave me in peace."

"Well then, I'll need to get a passport," I say, picturing our hotel room looking out on the Seine.

"Fine. You can apply for one tomorrow."

A rotten smell sweeps along the corridor, and I jerk my head back in disgust.

"That's the woman from number 32," I tell her. "She must be taking out the cat litter. She lets it build up too long before cleaning it out."

Alice can't smell it.

"It's coming from down there," I say, pointing to the far end of the corridor. I smile again as I open my door and feel Alice's hand on my arm.

"I wouldn't have survived this without you," she says.

I nod and close the door behind me. Blessedly, the stench from the cat litter has faded, but as I walk down the hallway it is replaced by the first traces of a scent I thought I had put behind me: the smell of bergamot.

TWENTY-SIX

"Not everyone should be allowed access to the keys to the apartments, Connor." I hear my voice bouncing off the walls of the basement. I sound hysterical.

"No one has access to the keys," Connor protests.

"I'm sorry," I reply, more calmly this time, I hope.

"I don't think anyone has gotten into your apartment."

"Oh really. How can you be so sure?"

"And if they have, you should call the police."

"What about a knife?"

"What *about* a knife?" he asks.

"You told me to get a knife, yet you don't believe anyone's broken into my apartment."

"Oh Christ, I was just messin' with you, Leah. This isn't one of the mystery novels the neighbors leave behind for me." He sounds upset, his Irish accent more prominent. "If anything, I was recommending it to Alice. She's the one with the stalker husband apparently."

I straighten up and try not to blink for at least a minute, while I think about what to say next. I make out an irritating whistle coming out of his nose as he breathes, together with body odor.

I hear the elevator ping and the scrape of the metal grille opening. It's Olivia, dragging a basket of dirty clothes.

"Let me help you," I say, turning my back on Connor, an unlit cigarette dangling uselessly from his mouth.

"What are you two talking about?" the old woman asks as we make our way into the laundry room.

"I want him to finish installing a new internal lock."

"Connor works when he feels like it, Leah. Or rather, when he has a drink inside him. He's a grouch."

"He's not that bad, Olivia," I say.

"You mark my words, a man who trifles around with a married woman is not to be trusted. He is nothing but a fool."

We step into the laundry room, and I feel for the light switch. The smell of detergent overwhelms me, so I say goodbye to Olivia.

"I'll come up for supper in a while," I tell her.

On my way back to the elevator, I hear a metallic thud.

"Connor?" I call out.

I peer inside the storage room, otherwise known as the bicycle cemetery, and see nothing but a tangle of aluminum and rubber tires. Someone has been listening to us. I step into the elevator and stare out through the oval window.

My conversation with Connor was disturbing. Now I know I must search for proof, something that will show I haven't invented the intrusions. There must be a reason for my fear. Someone is pursuing me; someone has invaded my home; someone is determined to rob me of sleep until I crumble and fear consumes me completely.

The daguerreotype.

"Who in their right mind would send something like that to a woman who can't see?" I say out loud.

I reach inside my purse and feel for it, but it's not there. Did I leave it at the bookstore with Mark? Suddenly I wonder if it ever existed at all. No one in the building has complained about broken mailboxes. How could I have lost it?

First I go up to my apartment; I can feel that my face is flushed. All the blood in my body is concentrated in my head. My bangs are damp. Now my hair looks even blacker. I stand in front of the mirror for several minutes. I walk out into the hallway feeling disoriented. What was I going to do?

An hour later, I head upstairs for dinner with Olivia and begin to realize that this is actually good news, right? If no one came into my apartment, that means no one held me down and touched me in my bed until I couldn't breathe. No one left me a daguerreotype of a blind girl. The bergamot man is an illusion.

And yet the smell of bergamot is a physical reality that has not gone away.

If the bergamot man doesn't exist, does that mean Alice and Michael don't either?

I follow the scent of freshly baked bread and enter Olivia's apartment. I open my eyes to capture an image of the place. I am curious to see if Olivia has made any changes since Mrs. Elman's death, like I did after Mom was taken to hospice. But I see every doily in its place, the same tablecloth spread out on the table, the bookshelves untouched and lined with dust. Olivia has kept it exactly as Mrs. Elman had it, as if she might show up at any moment. This isn't contentment. This is loneliness. She has kept up the tradition of Mrs. Elman's candles, which we light together. Olivia hums a tune as she sets the table. She seems relaxed, maybe even happy, despite her solitude.

The soup is hot. I see the steam linger on the bowl like a spiral that won't go away. I revel in the smell of baking bread. I savor it.

"Don't trust that Connor," she says out of the blue, though at least an hour has passed since we were down in the basement together. She's standing in the kitchen doorway. "Never trust a drunkard. I'm sure that instead of coffee, that man takes a shot of whiskey every morning."

"Don't exaggerate, Olivia. I think I was too hard on him. I had thought that he might leave the keys where anyone can find them. I worried that he might not lock up his office properly. But I think I was mistaken. At this point, I'm not sure of anything."

"Well, I hope you're not worrying too much about that Alice woman. You've seen how distressed she is because her husband left her, and you've ended up suffering on her behalf. But we shouldn't take on other people's troubles: we have enough of our own."

Confirmed: Alice exists.

"Alice will be fine now," I say with confidence. "I'm the one who needs to recover. I've barely slept."

"Alice is one of those women who have to have someone looking after them all the time," Olivia continues. "She must have been a popular girl at school, maybe even a class favorite. Now that she's separated from her husband, she's lost. Some people don't know how to be on their own and see danger where there isn't any. I think that's what is happening with her." She gives my hand a squeeze as she passes me on her way back to the kitchen.

No, I think to myself. That's not Alice at all. She is, in fact, independent and determined. She's smart, she's beautiful, she's everything I wish I could be. She escaped small-town life and moved to New York all on her own. She abandoned her studies because she found the man she wanted to raise a family with. She traveled the world with him, until his drinking pushed her away. She will do anything now to escape him.

"Olivia, it's not easy dealing with an abusive husband," I clarify.

"There's no man alive who would dare lift a finger to me!" she growls.

I feel my cell phone vibrate in my pocket. It's a message from Alice: *Tomorrow we're going to an exhibit. You'll like it.*

I should say no, that I already have plans. But I never have plans.

An hour later, I say goodbye to Olivia.

I feel clean, clearheaded, as if I have been able to remove my worries with soap and water. Alice texts me again. It's the passport application link.

I decide to sleep in peace, without fear. I lie down and before I close my eyes, I write to Alice: *Sleep well. See you tomorrow.*

The next day I wake up refreshed, full of energy. I print out the forms and start filling them out carefully so as not to make any mistakes. When I'm done, I search in my old bedroom's closet for a box that contains important documents. I open it and the first thing I see is my father's death certificate: *Overdose.*

Underneath it are my parents' birth certificates; mine is at the bottom.

I put on my dad's navy-blue blazer and head out to the Ivy League Stationers & Printers on Broadway and 116th Street. Each time I pass by, I see on the sidewalk the poster advertising passport photos: In Business Since 1978.

The man behind the counter, when he sees me come in, smiles as if he knows me. He approaches me and takes me by the arm.

"How can I help you?"

"I'm applying for a passport."

"Photos! You need a good photographer. Let's see, sit here." He points to a stool. I close my eyes and let him take me there.

"Ready?"

I open my eyes and feel the guy hovering over me.

"Your ears have to be uncovered."

I don't react.

The guy carefully places my hair behind my right ear. "That's it." A flash and I jump.

"Give me a few minutes," he says.

I remain static. I open and close my eyes and see on the wall in front of me several passport photos taped side by side. Down at the end, I recognize Alice's face.

"Here you go."

I pay and head to the post office on 112th Street and mail the form.

Alice also applied for her passport recently. I thought hers was still valid. Maybe Michael held on to it and she had to declare it was lost. Perhaps she's planning to run away.

I get home exhausted and dive into bed.

TWENTY-SEVEN

I should have stayed home, but we're already in a taxi. I knew this was a mistake after waking up with horrible stomach cramps and a fever. It felt like a monster was devouring my insides. There were no smells in the apartment. No sounds either.

I remember going to the bathroom and slumping down on the cold tile floor. On the verge of a panic attack, I vomited several times. Something was doing a number on my stomach. I sprinkled cold water on my face, rinsed out my mouth, and filled a bowl with ice cubes. I craved the cold. My lips were dry and cracked. I pushed a small ice cube under my tongue and let it melt.

I felt a little better after that and went back to bed, piling up several pillows to keep my head raised. I was shivering. I tried to drive away all the old bad thoughts and guilty feelings. I was running late. I got ready as fast as I could.

Now, riding in the taxi with Alice, I begin to nod off.

"Couldn't sleep last night either, Leah?" she asks me.

"I'm a little dizzy," I reply, leaning my head against the window. "Is it far?"

"We should have taken the subway. The traffic is dreadful at this time of day."

"We could walk."

"But I can see you're very tired."

"Don't worry about me. Let the taxi get as close as possible, and we can walk from there. Besides, the car is making my head spin." I take a hairclip out of my bag and pull my hair back into a low bun.

I look up, and Alice is smiling at me.

"I love it when you put your hair up. It brings out your freckles," she says, and lightly pokes the tip of my nose with her index finger.

"Thanks," I say shyly.

We get out of the taxi at Eighth Avenue and 48th Street and head east. I walk quickly, trying to get through the noise and the bodies crashing into me. Now we're in the middle of Times Square. A trail of light covers the skyscrapers and turns the cars into a shiny, freezing sea. I close my eyes and lean on Alice.

"Almost there," she says.

We enter through glass doors and step onto an escalator at the Marriott Hotel. I allow myself to be led, as I used to when my mother was alive. I take faltering steps, tapping with my new white stick as I go. I can sense people looking at me with curiosity.

"I've got the tickets, we can go in," Alice shouts triumphantly.

"I'm sorry, I could have paid for them."

"You're my guest, Leah. Come on." She takes my arm. "Michael collected daguerreotypes, and some were very valuable. These photos fascinate me. I love coming up with stories about the people in them."

I shudder. Then it must have been Michael who left the image of a blind girl in my mailbox. Michael.

We step into another room, where piano music is playing. The notes stretch out and then stop in a way that makes the air vibrate. People are entering the room silently. When I open my eyes, I am standing in front of a poster: The Daguerreian Society.

"They meet every year," Alice explains. "Collectors and dealers come from all over the world."

I am soon enveloped by the smells of camphor, dust, and sweat. The daguerreotypes, mostly presented in groups of ten within a single frame, are very small, and from a distance are nearly indecipherable. Each photograph is displayed at a different height, so that you must stop and look up, then down, before moving on to the next. Some people are using magnifying glasses to examine all the details of the century-old images. In the center of the room is a table where you can sign up for an auction.

I find I am having to blink constantly to discern the space around me.

"Don't you think they're lovely?" Alice asks from behind my shoulder. I am too overwhelmed to answer. "Leah, are you all right?"

"Where have you brought me?" I want to ask but instead I nod and continue moving through the exhibit. I open and close my eyes as I go from one daguerreotype to the next. I don't stop to examine: the details do not interest me. I am searching for a girl with white hair, dressed in lace. A child with no eyes.

"Is the crowd bothering you?" asks Alice. "The thing is, I feel safer surrounded by strangers."

I come to a halt in front of an image of a woman dressed entirely in black. She is wearing a fancy hat and has a stern look on her face. I'm not especially interested in the photograph, but several other spectators are admiring it.

"This is my favorite," I hear a man say behind me. "She must have been in front of the camera a long while, maybe having to hold her breath. Then they had to find the exact combination of mercury and silver to process the image. It was like alchemy," I hear him say. I imagine he is tall with gray hair.

"Why did you bring me here?" I ask Alice suddenly.

"I'm sorry, I thought it might interest you, but if you like, we can go."

"Why would photographs like this interest me?"

"Okay, let's go. I didn't mean to—"

"I'm a bit confused today," I say, interrupting her. "I'm the one who's sorry. Let's look at the items they're auctioning off before we leave."

We push forward into the crowd heading for the auction, and I spot a daguerreotype on display under a glass dome. A beam of light shines on it, revealing an odd set of faces. It appears to be a family of five: father, mother, and three children. A boy has a dog on his lap. Everyone is dressed in black, except for the baby, who is in white.

"Why do they have their eyes closed?" I ask under my breath, to no one in particular.

"Even the dog does."

"The children had died of cholera," I hear a woman's voice explain. "The parents posed for the photograph as if they too had died. According to our research, the parents took their own lives not long after the image was taken."

"How horrible," Alice whispers to me.

A man standing next to her cuts in: "It's a well-nigh perfect piece. And so is the size. It's rare to come across such a large daguerreotype."

"I think we ought to go," says Alice nervously.

We make our way out of the exhibit quickly, Alice pulling me behind her.

TWENTY-EIGHT

We eat together that evening at a pizzeria packed with tourists. I wonder why we couldn't have gone back uptown, but I get the feeling Alice wants to stay out of the neighborhood for as long as possible. We take the subway back to Mont Cenis.

Connor is standing outside the building, smoking a cigarette as usual, but disappears through the side door to his cave before we reach the entrance.

When we get to the third floor, I discreetly sniff for any trace of the bergamot fragrance. There is none. Alice hesitates as she introduces the key to her lock, so I invite her in for a cup of tea.

The aroma of chamomile with orange blossom floods the living room. I grab Antonia's amber jar of Heavenly Waters and let one, two, three drops fall inside. A little more. Maybe it was too much, but I can tell it's helping Alice relax. Sitting on the sofa, she rests her head on my shoulder. I look down, and the chamomile leaves have formed a perfect eye at the bottom of my cup.

I take a sip of my tea. When I blink, the eye has disintegrated.

"Why don't you go home and spend some time with your family?" I suggest.

"That's not an option."

Alice gets up from the sofa and goes into the kitchen to put her empty teacup in the sink. At one point, I see she's put her hand up to her forehead. I decide not to ask about the cousin in Philadelphia.

"Headache?" I ask.

"I don't feel very well," she says. "The stress, I think. But going back home would be hell. That town stifles me. Besides, I don't trust my mother. She'd likely take his side, blame me for the breakup. Try to convince me to stay with him. She's spent her life blaming me for my father leaving us, because he said he couldn't bear me crying as a baby. She claims that's why she was left on her own."

She stops to give me a kiss on the cheek on her way to the front door. Then rummages through her bag.

"I've been wanting you to have this for some time," she says, thrusting a key into my hand. "It's a spare key to my apartment. You never know . . ."

I hear Alice step inside her apartment and close the door behind her. I walk over and place my hands on my side of the wall, flare my nostrils, and listen. Alice is alone. She is safe.

I go to the bathroom and pause in front of the mirror. Images flash through my mind of the family in the daguerreotype. I imagine the husband and wife posing beside their dead children, forced into stillness, minute after unbearable minute. The slightest movement would have ruined the image. I imagine the smell of the mercury vapors coming off the copper plates.

With my eyes wide open, I move my head from side to side. The mirror looks like it's melting. I blink and freeze but can't see myself reflected in the mirror. Instead, I see Alice's face gazing back at me. An instant later, the image fades, and the mirror becomes dark. Deep inside the mirror, I see Alice lying in a sea of blood. She is surrounded by red emulsions of mercury and silver. Just like a daguerreotype.

TWENTY-NINE

I'm afraid Michael will once again pick my lock or find a way in. Another sleepless night. Even so, I answer Antonia's phone call, careful not to worry her: Yes, I've eaten. Yes, I've slept. I'm even reading a book that has nothing to do with blindness, a novel about the photographer Louis Daguerre. No, I haven't seen Alice, she's been gone for two days. Yes, the apartment is tidy. Yes, I've been to see Dr. Allen.

I say all of this to Antonia, but only some of it is true. I haven't visited Dr. Allen for two or three weeks. I haven't slept for several nights, I'm not sure how many. Alice has disappeared, I'm not sure where. She didn't tell me, and I didn't ask. Why doesn't Alice trust me? Maybe she is trying to protect me.

I am anxious. I wish I could disappear into a book, but I can't concentrate.

My hair feels heavy with grease. A shower would do me good; I'm so tense. Perhaps I should shout, jump up and down, or stretch. I must do something, or I will go mad. A shower. Yes, a shower will do me good.

I open my eyes, and I am lying in bed. I must have fallen asleep. My phone says it's after midnight. I hear voices coming from downstairs or maybe from outside.

I have a bad feeling about that woman.

Is the voice coming from apartment 31? Is it Mrs. Bemer?

I've seen a man come and go from her apartment. He stays for hours. I don't think it's her husband. It's a young fellow.

With a jolt, it occurs to me it could be Pete. No, no, he's in DC. Unless he was lying to me. And he has never smelled like bergamot. Still, he could have met Alice when he was delivering my dinner one night. *Stop it,* I tell myself, *you're being absurd.*

I saw her walking into the park at night. That woman isn't right in the head.

So it wasn't a dream. Alice was in the park in a red dress.

She goes around all the time with Leah. I'll bet she wants that poor blind girl's money.

Poor blind girl. Why must they always see me as that?

I hear the front door handle move. The metal creaks. Someone is trying to force the lock, but I know they can't get in: the internal lock was finally installed, and the safety chain is in place. I live in an impenetrable fortress.

I get out of bed. The hallway is filled with ghosts from the daguerreotypes. The door to my apartment shines like a mirror. In it, I see Alice's reflection, her face a mass of wrinkles. Closing my eyes, I run to the French doors, open them, and allow the icy raindrops to sweep in.

Down by the park, underneath the streetlight, I see Alice and Connor standing. They are holding hands, looking up at me. They turn to each other and kiss. I blink, and Michael has joined them, but he has no face. The space where it should be is blank. The smell of bergamot floats through the air and snakes its way up the Boston ivy until it reaches my balcony. I am enveloped by the cursed smell, but I am able to make out a picture of Michael in my mind. Just as his eyes are coming into focus, Alice throws a white veil over my head, blocking my vision.

I wake up with a start and realize I've been dreaming again.

THIRTY

I'm entangled in my white comforter, naked, my hair damp from sweat. Books are strewn about the floor; an empty water bottle is on the bed. How many hours have I slept? The last time I looked out the window, it was dawn; the sun is setting now. I finally feel rested. I can't remember the last time I ate, but I am full of energy. I climb out of bed and fill the bath with hot water. The steam is a solid mass floating on the uneven surface. I pour in some violet salts. I see my face reflected in the circles created by the tiny crystals.

I submerge myself completely in the tub. I hold my breath under the water, open my eyes, and return to the surface.

It's time to resume my usual routine: read, write, take photos, post online, go to Book Culture, see Dr. Allen. Antonia will be back next week, and everything will return to normal.

I hope Alice will leave the city for good. That would be for the best.

After my bath, I make myself a cup of tea and curl up on the couch in the living room to read. I pick up a book at random: *All the Light We Cannot See*.

I once had a father like the one in this book. He showed me every street corner of the city. But that was before I was blind like the book's heroine.

I run to the door when my supper arrives and am met by an older man smelling of tobacco and garlic.

Hours pass, and I eventually fall asleep on the couch with my book open across my lap. A dull thud awakens me. I open my eyes but can't hear anything. There are no voices; everyone in the building must be asleep. I close the book and walk toward my bedroom, when I am shaken by a crash. It sounds like someone is trying to knock down the wall in the front hallway.

The floor is shaking; I feel the vibration on the soles of my feet. I try to locate a voice behind the commotion. Nothing. I continue walking toward my bedroom with my hand flat against the wall. I sit on my bed and concentrate with my eyes closed. I flare my nostrils: all I need is a scent to ignite all my senses. I wait for another bang; the silence is unnerving. My palms are clammy. I can hear every heartbeat on my fingertips, in my chest, at my temples.

I lie down and try something else. I decide to block out all my senses and forget what I just heard on the far side of the wall. The noise could have come from above or below me, or maybe something happened out on the street. It only sounded like it came from next door. It wouldn't be the first time I got something wrong. Not even superpowers are foolproof.

I get into bed and switch on the air-conditioning to its highest speed, hoping the sound of the motor will drown out any other noise, but it is too late: by now all my senses are on alert.

I notice a slight vibration in the oak floorboards. All I hear is the air-conditioning and my heartbeats. I count them one by one to calm myself.

A shout startles me. It is followed by footsteps on hardwood. Another shout, and the sound of blows, this time against the wall. I tremble under the comforter; I don't want to listen. I don't want any of this. Until I hear my name:

"Leah!"

Now I hear sobbing, and someone trying to call out.

I run to my entrance hall. The shouting is coming from the other side of the wall.

Silently, I try to determine where the movements are coming from.

"Leah!" I hear again. A call for help.

This isn't happening, I tell myself. I'm asleep. I'm completely alone.

"Let go of me!" I hear. I can make out the struggle, the blows against the wall and the wooden floorboards. A body thrown against the wall makes the floor shake again.

Then silence, again. I need one more sign to know if this is real, or if it's a nightmare. If this is all really happening, surely I would hear other neighbors stirring. Surely these loud noises would have woken someone else up too.

Another muffled shout: "Help me!"

In a flash, I run back to my bedroom and get the key that Alice gave me. I open the drawer and grab the knife. There is no time to calculate or think. As though guided by some external force, I run from my bedroom out into the hallway and out my front door, and I push the key into my neighbor's lock. I step inside. In the darkness, with the bright light of the hallway behind me, I can make out only a silhouette.

First image: Alice with her head pressed against the wall, scarcely breathing. A thin line of blood down her forehead. On top of her is a man lying facedown. His right arm is flat against the dividing wall; the other is bent up to his face.

Second image: Alice's eyes are open and terrified.

Third image: Alice is pushing the man's body off of her.

Alice is screaming words I can't make out. I launch myself, knife in hand, at the man's neck. One, two, three, four . . . I count every stab of the metal blade until I reach twenty-four. Only then do I let go of the knife and collapse into a sea of blood.

Alice is still screaming. All I smell is iron and rust.

THIRTY-ONE

The last time I celebrated my birthday was when I was eight. Mom took me to see *The Lion King*. Now I see Antonia come in, staring at the candle burning timidly on a small cake topped with butter-cream. *I'm already twenty-nine years old*, I say to myself. She is standing in the doorway flanked by two nurses, the receptionist, and the doctor.

"Did you think I'd forget?" she says with a smile as she steps into the room. I blow out the candle. "Don't say your wish out loud if you want it to come true, my girl."

I hug the nurses and lean on Antonia as the doctor holds out his hand to guide me. It's time to say goodbye to the green hospital room where I spent the summer, fall, and winter.

Exiting the clinic, we are met with a blast of freezing air. A car is waiting for us, and we quickly seek shelter inside.

"I should have brought you a warmer coat," Antonia says, a little breathless from the walk through the parking lot.

"I'm fine, Antonia. I needed a bit of fresh air."

When the car sets off, I reach back and pull my hair into a braid. My hair now reaches the middle of my back.

"Look at how your hair has grown in eight months; you need a haircut," Antonia says. "If you like, tomorrow I can go to the hairdresser with you."

I smile at her kindness, but I need to be on my own. I need to start over.

"I talked to Dr. Allen. He thinks you're going to be all right. He says it's time you went home, but he's expecting to see you at his office on Monday."

"I know, I spoke to him this morning."

"This is what you wanted, isn't it? Now you don't seem so—"

"Antonia, I'm fine. Of course it's what I wanted. I'm really looking forward to being home."

"That Mont Cenis . . . I don't know why you don't put the apartment up for sale. It would be good for you."

"Maybe someday. Right now I have to look into selling Olivia's apartment."

"Poor Olivia."

"I couldn't say goodbye to her," I whisper. I wish I could have been there for her.

"She was very old. And we old folk always have one foot on the other side."

At Mont Cenis, the driver hastens to help me, but I open the car door determinedly. The avenue is busier than usual, and so I tap my stick against the sidewalk. There is a slight evening mist, the sun is setting, and the spotlight over the building entrance has been turned on. I pause to look at the facade and the withered ivy, with only its roots and dry stems clinging to the brickwork.

The elevator smells of fresh varnish, and I flinch every time the bell rings.

When we reach the third floor, I step out first, leaving Antonia behind.

"The family who bought number 34 is charming," Antonia calls after me. "It's a young couple with a five-year-old boy. They haven't finished moving in yet, but they will soon. For now you'll be able to sleep in peace."

There is no trace of any smell of the past. Antonia has scrubbed hard with disinfectant to remove anything that might awaken my memory.

I move cautiously toward the French doors and look down at the steps to the park.

Snowflakes dot my view.

"Let's hope it's the last of the season," says Antonia as she strokes my hair. She goes into the kitchen and switches on the light. "I'll make us some supper."

I get out my cell phone and take a photo of the empty stairs.

"You could do with a shower," Antonia suggests. She'll get no argument from me.

Before entering the bathroom, I look around my bedroom. Stacks of books still line all four walls.

I leave my phone on the bedside table, still showing the photo of the stairs. I start to undress, and while I search my closet for something to wear, my cell begins to vibrate.

Startled, I run to see who might be calling. The screen shows "Private Number." At the fourth vibration, I pick up:

"Hullo," I whisper. On the other end of the line, there is nothing and I hang up. Sitting naked on the edge of my bed, I feel dizzy and the books start to spin around me, but I keep my eyes open. I hear Antonia drop a kitchen utensil, and the noise breaks the spell. I step calmly into the bathroom, leaving my fear behind. Nothing and no one can intimidate me.

The hot water courses down my face and chest. I want to be rid of every molecule of my confinement. The moment has come to begin afresh, to forget. The white foam stays imprinted on my eyes even as it disappears down the plughole.

When I've finished bathing, Antonia is seated at the table, waiting for me. She didn't want to rush me even though our supper has grown cold. We eat without exchanging a word. The only sound is of the cutlery on our plates.

"I left the envelope with your passport on the kitchen shelf," Antonia finally says. "I didn't know you had requested it."

I smile.

"Leah, you know you did the right thing," Antonia continues.

I don't respond. Antonia stands shakily and takes our plates back to the kitchen.

"You reacted as anybody would have done. You shouldn't feel guilty." I start organizing the books on the dining room shelves.

"Besides, it was Connor who warned you to protect yourselves. He himself said as much. We all knew what poor Alice was going through. Luckily, you're never going to have to see her again. The best thing now is to forget, and to do that you need to realize you did nothing wrong, that it was all in self-defense. Who knows what might have happened to her and to you? I can't even bear thinking about it."

Antonia walks over and wraps me in her arms. She feels strong when she holds me, but I can tell that she still hasn't recovered from her heart attack months earlier. I wish I could take care of her for once.

"Wouldn't you like me to stay with you tonight?"

"No, really, I'll be fine."

"Okay then, give me a kiss good night."

"I'll come to the door with you."

We embrace again, and Antonia kisses me on the forehead.

"Ay, my child," she sighs, caressing my face with both hands, following the trail of my freckles with her thumbs. "We got rid of someone who could have hurt you tremendously. That man was no good. Now you'll be able to sleep in peace. We'll talk tomorrow. Get some rest."

I close the door gently, turn the lock, and put up the safety chain.

Antonia is right. I did the only thing I knew to do in that moment. And it's true that Alice would be dead now if it weren't for me.

There's only one problem. The man I killed didn't smell of bergamot.

THIRTY-TWO

I spend the next few mornings throwing out all the books on blindness. They have fulfilled their role, and now I want to bring some fresh air into the apartment. Mom had bought them like so many white sticks, until there was a whole collection of them. I don't need them anymore. From now on I will buy books about photography. I want to learn about composition and light. I want to play with the tones and colors around me. Living in a world of static images, I want to capture them digitally, to write and paint with light.

It is still cold in the city, with fitful sunlight and heavy clouds, but the ivy is starting to produce timid green shoots.

"You know Boston ivy is poisonous, don't you?" Connor asks when he sees me gazing at the front of the building.

"I don't think anyone would try to eat one of the leaves, do you?"

"The seeds. Those dry seeds you see me sweeping up are what's dangerous," the super replies. "I'm glad you're back."

"It was time."

"You know you can count on me, Leah," he says earnestly.

"I know." And I mean it. "I'm going to need you when I start clearing out Olivia's apartment."

"Poor woman, she died alone in the hospital."

"Connor, we all end up dying alone."

"I visited her a few times. The last time she didn't even recognize me."

"Antonia told me her dementia accelerated after she was left on her own," I said. "That is worse than death itself."

"At least she died untroubled, knowing you were okay and that nothing had happened to you. She was concerned about you the whole time, asked how you were getting on in the hospital . . . in the clinic. She bought all the newspapers."

"Thanks, Connor. I have to get on, or I'll be late."

I try to slip away quickly, but a dog approaches and starts sniffing at my stick. I head in the opposite direction, but the dog insists on following me until its owner tugs on its leash.

Clusters of students are lying on the Columbia University lawns, sunbathing like it's summer.

I dig around my bag for a scarf, bump into a young man, and drop my stick. I hear it roll away and the boy chase after it. When I open my eyes, there are shadows everywhere. It's been a long time since I've been outside; I'm still not accustomed to natural light.

The boy returns with my stick, takes hold of my hands, and places it between my fingers.

He thinks I'm blind. I smile and continue on my way with my eyes closed. The neighborhood feels entirely new to me.

Farther south, on the east side of Broadway, are the fruit and vegetable sellers. Some look at me; others greet me as if they recognize me. All the way to Book Culture, it's as if I'm being examined. Which, let's face it, I probably am. My story was covered extensively in the newspapers.

Look who's here, I overhear one of the store assistants whisper as I stop to look at the facade of St. John the Divine and get my bearings. *Didn't she go to prison?*

No. She fell into a coma or something.

I heard she couldn't speak.

She was in the hospital for a while, and then she was sent to a psychiatric clinic. That's what I read online anyway.

Poor girl . . .

Poor girl.

A violent burst of light causes me to miss the rest of the dialogue. The bell rings when I unlatch the door. Now they will keep quiet. When I open my eyes, I see faces staring back at me. Their silhouettes look flat in the semidarkness; the books are like floating blocks.

"Good morning. Is Mark here today?"

"Oh, Mark doesn't work here anymore. When he graduated . . ."

I stumble closer to the cashier table. Sounds fade away, and the light intensifies. It hurts my eyes.

"I could try getting his phone number for you," the other assistant says, no doubt registering my shock. I am overwhelmed by the fabricated rose scent of her perfume.

"No, thank you . . . don't worry about it," I reply, and climb the stairs, forgetting that the photography section is on the floor below. In my flustered state, I can think only of escaping up to the second floor. I see my armchair under the window has disappeared. In fact, there is nowhere to sit. The children's section has expanded; there are shelves of toys. Hearing a hubbub of shrieks, I come to a halt in the middle of the room. The walls begin to whirl around me, but I stand absolutely still, clutching my stick so firmly it nearly pierces the floor.

A mother with a baby in her arms sees me.

"The last time I saw you in here I was still pregnant," she says.

"I don't recall having seen you," I say back.

The woman thinks I'm being funny. Blind girl humor. She replies with a timid little laugh as she cradles the baby with her whole body.

I wonder what would happen if I pointed out that not only can I see but I stabbed my neighbor's husband to death. How would she react? Yes, I did it in self-defense; I have a witness to prove it. But that does not exonerate me from the crime: I am a murderer. I stabbed him twenty-four times.

How about if I also explain that the blood gushed out of the wound like a river, that the smell was overwhelming, that the man didn't even react to my attack, as if he somehow had been expecting it all along? Here I am, ready or not!

I could also tell her that I was never in a coma. I suffered a nervous breakdown like I did when I was eighteen. I spent maybe a month completely disoriented; little by little, I recovered in a clinic that is really an asylum for another seven months. Did the newspapers publish that? How much of my private life is now public? All that, and I killed the wrong man. Yes, I killed Michael, but the bergamot man is still out there haunting me.

I open my eyes and look at the baby once more. Without glancing at the mother, I say: "I think you need to change the diaper."

With that, I head for the stairs. As I descend, I hear the woman asking her baby in a singsong voice, as if she's reciting a nursery rhyme, "How did she know that, if she can't see, baby boy? How did the blind lady know that?"

THIRTY-THREE

That evening, I fall asleep on the sofa with all the lights on and am awakened by footsteps in the corridor. Soft, scurrying footsteps. I run over to the front door and find a piece of paper has been pushed underneath it. It smells of fresh ink. I assume it's from Connor, a notice about building maintenance or some new regulation, or maybe a menu from a local restaurant. Or possibly it's a summons from the NYPD informing me they are going to reopen the case, renew the interviews, call witnesses. I will have to relive the scene and the image I can't get out of my head; worse still, the smell of iron and rust that only a whiff of roasted coffee beans is able to suppress.

Picking up the piece of paper, I see a photograph of my building printed in the center. It's been superimposed onto a field of blooming lavender. Looking at this, no one would ever know it's located in one of the world's most populated cities. It looks like it's nestled in Provence, the perfect getaway from the bustle of modern life. I take the photo back to my bedroom and see that it's a flyer from the real estate agent who sold Alice's apartment. After what happened, the owner didn't want to keep it, not even as an investment property.

I get a glass of cold water to moisten my lips, but don't drink any.

Behind the strong smell of ink on the glossy paper, I can distinguish hints of gardenia and lemon. The leaflet was left by a woman. At the bottom right is a blurred photograph of a smiling blonde, her lips so pumped up they look like they might burst. Apparently, Mary Reed can sell my apartment "for a price you never dreamed of!" She is an expert not only on this building but on all of Morningside Heights, and claims to have sold number 34 in record time.

I'm curious to know if the apartment was sold at the asking price, or if my crime reduced its value.

The Miller family moves in on Friday morning. By four in the afternoon, all the furniture, boxes, and suitcases are inside the apartment. When I go downstairs, Connor is removing the protective wall and floor coverings from the elevator.

"Those people had a ton of stuff," he complains. "I don't know how they managed to fit in everything they brought."

According to Connor, the Millers paid a contractor to restore the original wood archways and crown moldings; they installed new parquet floors. "The place was torn up pretty bad," he said, choosing his words carefully. They are outfitting the maid's room for an au pair.

Connor seems put out. They've made him work more than he is accustomed to in this building full of old-timers and a blind girl. They keep calling him, asking him questions he doesn't have the answers to. I assume they are asking about me: if I could be a danger to the child, if I have been badly affected, if I cry out at night due to nightmares.

In fact, for months now I have been sleeping for more than eight hours a night, untroubled by dreams or nightmares. I sleep like the dead.

Since my return, the only thing that remains vivid is my memory of what happened that night with Alice and her husband, but I am convinced that even that will evaporate eventually.

"Why don't you keep number 54 and sell number 33?" Connor suggests. "Mrs. Elman's apartment is bigger than yours."

"What do I need a bigger apartment for?"

"Or keep both of them. You don't have to sell anything at all, do you?"

I don't reply and can feel Connor watching me as I walk down the front steps and onto the street.

"Things will get back to normal, Leah. Give it some time," I hear him say.

THIRTY-FOUR

Mary Reed is a vision in pale yellow. Her hair and pantsuit match perfectly. Her enormous lips are a dull, sticky pink. She strides into number 54 after a long day showing other apartments to people she calls "looky-loos," who "don't have enough in their bank accounts to make an offer."

"There's still a lot of work to do here," I say as I show her around Mrs. Elman's place. It's dark and smells of damp, dust, and piles of old newspapers. "Connor is going to clear it out for me."

"Great. And it could do with a coat of paint, couldn't it? With this much space, someone's going to snap it up in no time," she says, snapping her fingers for emphasis.

Mary heads over to the kitchen and opens the cabinets, sniffs around in the drawers and the cupboards. I lose her. I see diffuse images of her wandering into a bedroom, pulling on a rug to examine the wood floor. She hauls a potted plant to the side and groans when she sees a water stain.

"The first thing Connor needs to do is to get rid of this thing," she calls out, pointing to the plant. "It's ruining the floor." But something else is bothering her. "I'm going out to buy air freshener. It smells like death in here."

"Here's the key," I say, extending my hand. "I'm staying a bit longer, but feel free to come and go as you like anytime."

"Thanks, I'll do that. Come to think of it, I should make an appearance at my office for a bit. I'll come back tomorrow with the air freshener."

I sigh with relief when Mary leaves. I look all around the apartment until my eyes come to rest on a white envelope sitting on the kitchen table. My name is spelled out on the front of it. Olivia must have left it here before she was taken to the hospital. Inside is the Star of David on a gold chain that belonged to Mrs. Elman. I search for an inscription. If there was one, the letters have worn away. Also on the table are two piles of newspapers and clippings from magazines. On the wall calendar, July 7 is circled, as if time had stopped that day. The day I killed Michael.

It's hot in the apartment, as if summer still resides here. I go over to the calendar, breathe in as deeply as I can, close my eyes, and try to summon up Olivia. The faint essence of violet water and cinnamon fills my nostrils.

Connor dialed 911 when Olivia didn't answer his knocks—how could she have responded if she'd been lying on the wooden floor for hours? Her brain ran out of oxygen for who knows how many minutes. Olivia was alive, but she and I know that a person can die before that, long before the heart stops beating. She spent several days in a hospital, then went from the hospital to the hospice and from the hospice to the morgue.

The dim light from the ceiling chandelier makes the room seem darker. Several of the bulbs have gone out, and what little light there is falls on the far side of the table, away from the newspapers. As I move them closer to me, one of the clippings drifts to the floor and falls underneath a chair.

Picking up the piece of paper, I sit down, blink, and am staring at Alice's face, though after all these months I must admit I barely recognize her.

In the photograph, she is wearing a tight-fitting black dress and high heels. Her hair is shorter and shows off her perfect jawline. Her bangs create a line across her forehead. She has on a pair of dark sunglasses and is carrying a square leather handbag. She appears to be trying to avoid the camera, as if she has been pursued by the photographer. The caption describes her as being at her late husband's funeral, receiving condolences from friends and Michael Turner's family, as well as colleagues from his legal practice.

I begin sifting through the rest of the articles. With each blink, I see a new headline: "Lawyer Turned Wife Beater Perishes," "Bloodbath on the Upper West Side," "Park Avenue Predator Becomes Prey," "Blind Woman Saves Park Avenue Heiress," "The Last Thrust." They go on and on. I feel strangely detached from all of it, as if it has nothing to do with me.

In a glossy *People* magazine piece, a few of Michael's colleagues accuse him of being "abusive," "impulsive," and "foul-mouthed." According to them, he had recently started drinking again and frequently came to work reeking of alcohol.

Michael's sister, however, presented a different picture: "He was incapable of hurting anyone . . . he stopped drinking five years ago . . . it was a relapse, nothing more . . . in the end, addiction is an illness, isn't it . . . it just shows what harm alcohol can do."

The article lists a number of high-profile cases Michael won as an attorney and several charities for which he was a board member. It also says the married couple had signed a prenuptial agreement. According to Michael Turner's lawyer, "he couldn't understand how Alice, a girl from a small town who had no independent means of support, could be so crazy as to leave him and accept a divorce that left her without a cent from the multimillion-dollar family trust account." A stipulation of the agreement, however, was that Alice would not receive alimony unless they had a child. That child never arrived. Or Michael made sure of it. I think back to what Alice told me when we were at Washington Square Park.

Alice did get the Park Avenue penthouse, which she and Michael had bought for four million dollars after they returned from their honeymoon. That price was nothing for the location, the *Times* real estate section pointed out, although the renovation cost several times the original sum. Michael's sister, according to a *New York Post* article, had no intention of claiming any part of the fortune gained from its sale, on condition that Alice did not try to claim damages and sue the family. I see a quote from Alice in *New York* magazine: "That's fine with me. I didn't marry Michael for the money anyway. All I want is to leave New York and never come back."

I go to the sink for a glass of water, return to the table, and continue reading in the gloom. I pause at one of the close-up photos that shows the widow staring at the camera. Is that triumph I see? Perhaps. But mostly, she looks tired and sad and beautiful.

After a while, I begin to notice that in most cases, only portions of the articles are here. It seems Olivia cut out paragraphs, almost always from the middle of the text, and sometimes at the end, as if she was editing or censoring what was written. I notice it happening whenever my name comes up. The articles that are intact praise me as a heroine. The ones that are sliced and diced must have criticized my method of defense. Olivia didn't want me to see those negative comments, only the good.

Everyone, including Michael Turner's family, accepted the conclusions of the police, according to the *Daily News*. They did not press any charges against me or Alice.

Vanity Fair published photographs of the Turner couple on their honeymoon in Europe. They look happy, young, and glamorous. In one photo, the only one that captures him looking directly at the camera, there is a slight smile on his face, but it's closer to a smirk. I feel like I'm seeing him for the first time. This is the man I killed.

Michael, I want to say to him. *You were not a good man, but I didn't mean to kill you.* And the smile in the photograph fades. Deep in his eyes I see fear. What I can't figure out is if he's afraid *of* me or *for* me.

Picking up the last newspaper, I see a page that Olivia and her scissors must have missed. It's another *New York Post* piece. In the real estate section, she circled the headline: "Alice Turner Sells Park Avenue Apartment for 20 Million Dollars; Bids Adieu to Big Apple."

THIRTY-FIVE

It is almost midnight and I can't sleep. I am afraid the insomnia is coming back. I try some breathing exercises, and tighten, then relax, my leg and arm muscles. There is no point trying to understand Alice now. She left the city without looking back, without even looking back at me, the blind girl who saved her. Maybe it's only now that Alice can begin her own process of recovery—alone, far away from everything, from photographers and reporters. Now that she's gained so much, she'll be able to do that.

I open my nightstand's drawer where I keep my passport. I carefully take it out, open it, and stop at my photo. It's as if I took that photo years ago and I don't recognize myself.

"Alice, we're not going to Paris anymore," I say out loud.

I jump out of bed and head to the dining room, where my laptop awaits. Suddenly, I feel the need to fill in the pieces that Olivia left behind. I want to know everything that was written about me.

I discover that I have become quite the celebrity on social media, even though I haven't posted anything in months. My Instagram profile, according to a digital news site, is one of the most visited. I even find photos of July 7. In a screenshot from a TV image, I see myself lying covered in blood and unconscious on a gurney. In another one, Alice's husband's body is in a black body bag. There is a shot of Alice in a state of panic, escorted by NYPD officers, and Connor giving an interview to reporters. My neighbor Mrs. Stein is covering her face. The Phillipses are hugging each other, crying.

#akinetopsia is trending on Twitter. Sites devoted to motion blindness have become popular, with thousands of hits. Several influencers have made videos explaining the illness, showing in images how a patient suffering from akinetopsia sees the world. There are explanations of the Greek origins of the word: *Akinesia: the lack of movement. Opsis: to see.*

As dawn arrives, I find the complete version of one article that Olivia edited. This one is different. Not only does it cover the awful details of the stabbing; it's a full exposé of me and my family.

Nothing in the article is new to me. In the photograph, my father looks like a ghost. It must be one of his last professional headshots before going bald; I recognize the drooping eyes, long nose, thin lips, broad forehead, and thinning hair. The long neck, big eyes. I see myself in him. Dad could spend time alone, with himself. Me too. Dad could read all night, like me.

Dad was an actor weary of waiting for his big break; he spent years studying the craft but mostly waited tables to make ends meet. The article explains that Daniel Anderson met Emily Thomas at a charity function at Columbia University. He was working that night for the caterer; she was there as a guest. They were a dynamic couple, the report says. Attractive, clever, and young. Within a few months, they were engaged.

Did he marry Mom for the money? Did she marry him for the excitement and fame she thought his life in the theater would bring? He never abandoned his dreams of becoming a well-respected actor, the article says. Thanks to his wife's trust fund and inherited Upper West Side apartment, he no longer had to wait tables, but his career never got any further than the limited circuit of off-

off-Broadway. Later came alcohol and depression and fighting at home. Though there is a quote from one of his actor friends that "being the dad to his daughter, Leah, was definitely the highlight of his life."

On my eighth birthday, Dad was at a rehearsal, and Mom took me to see *The Lion King* on Broadway. She had fallen in love with a book publishing executive and was planning to end her marriage, the article says. After the show we ate dinner at a restaurant and when we got home we entered the apartment quietly, in case Dad was asleep.

The article goes on to describe the "freak accident" that left me with akinetopsia. It reports that my father died of a drug overdose, and my mother's relationship ended. She never remarried, never traveled the world, but devoted the rest of her life to my care.

What the article doesn't describe is my foggy memory of that night. How I ran to the bathroom but found the door closed. When I opened it, a cold gust of air reeking of iron and rust hit me. And there was another fragrance. Stepping inside, I slipped on a sticky substance. Leaning over to switch the light on, I lost my balance. Blinded by the bright light, my eight-year-old body toppled, and I hit my head on the edge of the toilet bowl. Clutching at the glass shelf, I only managed to pull it down on top of me. There was glass everywhere, and, right in front of my eyes, a small amber bottle, its transparent contents dripping down on me, enveloping me in a citrusy, floral scent. The label on the bottle was still intact.

"Bergamot," I whisper.

I close my eyes, I try to relive the scene and I can't. Where was my mother at that moment? We'd come back from the theater together, laughing along the way; I was running ahead, skipping. Now she's no longer with me, she's abandoned me. I go up the stairs, walk down the hallway, and open the door. The apartment is dark. I enter the bathroom alone and step on glass. Suddenly, I sink into a sea of blood. It's dense, warm. I'm drowning and I want to survive—I can't let this defeat me. My legs, my arms feel heavy. My mouth dries up; my skin is permeated by the metallic smell. Now I'm covered by a dark sheet that prevents me from moving.

That is all I know of how I got the way I am. I remember nothing of *The Lion King*, or the meal, or my mother's face when she lifted me off the floor, covered in blood. Nor can I recall the days spent in the hospital. I remember only the string of sentences repeated ad nauseam by Dr. Allen:

"You'll be fine. Someday everything will return to normal. The damage is reversible. For now you have to learn how to survive."

So here I am. I have survived, but what did the doctor mean when he spoke of "normal"? Would my father ever come back? Would the world ever start moving again? Those were the questions I asked myself every night before going to sleep when I was a girl. And why does a blind girl need to sleep anyway? To add more darkness to the one she already has to bear?

Closing my eyes now, in my mind's eye my father's face overlaps with Alice's.

"Alice . . ." I call out, as the memory of a dinner with my parents before the world came to a stop flashes through my mind.

"The pillows smell of Daddy—everything smells of Daddy in our home," I said, sitting across from him.

"That's because I want you never to forget me," he replied with a smile.

"It's the tonic your father uses for his hair," Mom explained with an easy laugh. "He doesn't want to end up bald, so Antonia gave him one of her potions."

"It's bergamot," he said. "It's made from a fruit called bergamot."

I don't want to think about this anymore. Enough. I open Google and go to the International Center of Photography website. Among the course selections, there is a group of classes under Personal Vision. There I find The Art of Seeing. I write my name, my address, and my Instagram handle: @BlindGirlWhoReads. Sent.

I bang my computer shut and open my Instagram account on my iPhone.

When I click on my profile, I see I have more than 100,000 followers.

I can't get the bloody image of my father, lifeless, surrounded by broken glass, out of my mind. Poor Dad . . . I now walk to the bathroom, the same bathroom where I found him dying. I open the door and don't dare turn on the light. I close my eyes and can hear my father's voice dissolving in my memory, "Help me."

THIRTY-SIX

I'm standing inside the 116th Street subway station on the south-bound platform. An old man takes my arm without asking.

"Here comes the train," he shouts, as if I'm deaf as well.

"Thanks, I can manage on my own from here."

"No way. I'll help you get on and find a seat for you. Which stop do you want?"

"I change trains at Columbus Circle."

"Hmm, that's rather complicated."

"Don't worry, I'm used to it," I lie.

As we board the train, the man waves his hand at the other passengers, reserving the seat closest to the doors for me.

"Can somebody please let this girl know when the train has reached the Columbus Circle station?" he shouts to no one in particular.

"I can hear the announcement. Thanks," I insist.

Reaching the busy Columbus Circle station, I navigate with my eyes open, using my stick. It feels like I'm scaling a vast human wall, but I am able accomplish it with a surgeon's precision, hardly bumping into anyone. My goal is to find the orange line going downtown.

When I finally reach the Lower East Side, I head for the photography center, covering the distance in swift strides. I block my strong sense of smell so that I'm not overwhelmed by this new environment, enter, and am immediately disoriented by the bright overhead lights.

"I've come for my class," I announce to the young man at the front desk.

"Great," he says, with a notable lack of enthusiasm. "What is your instructor's name? Or do you have a course number handy?"

"The Art of Seeing," I answer.

Silence. He must think I'm joking. Me, eyes closed, gripping a white stick.

Nevertheless, he escorts me to the elevator.

The class is starting in ten minutes. We enter the classroom through a glass door.

"At the back, please. I prefer to sit in the last row."

The boy asks for my name, steps up to the front of the room, and reviews several sheets of paper to confirm my enrollment. The room fills up. Everyone is standing in front of me until I close my eyes. In my mind, the image loses color. They are all dressed in white, black, and gray. I make out a red handkerchief and a blue pocketbook. I can't smell them. I don't want to.

There are two teachers, Susan Nelson and Oscar Green. We can call them Susan and Oscar, they say. More than a class, it's a workshop. It's about the art of seeing, how we see what surrounds us with our cameras, how we give it a different life than the one it has when we filter it through our naked eyes. Everyone in the class is going to become a silent witness to everything that goes on around us each day. It doesn't matter which camera we use—it can be an iPhone or a Leica. The most important thing in class is our eyes.

Susan and Oscar are in the middle of putting together an exhibition for a gallery in Brooklyn; it's possible that some of the student work from this class could be shown there too. The exhibition will mix still and moving images. It's at the end of the semester and we're all invited.

Oscar asks us to introduce ourselves. My heart begins to race. I need to calm down, but to do that I must keep my eyes closed. I am sitting in the last row, but we are only about ten, maybe twelve, students. Surely everyone will assume I've fallen asleep. I'm already mortified.

One student talks about flowers, another about speed, another about street fashion. Then there's the guy who prefers images of objects, rather than people. "Art liberated from the ego is the only thing that interests me," he says. A quiet woman with a Russian accent wants to create a visual diary of her family, which consists of her, her cat, and her books. A younger man wants to document underground New York, the one nobody sees, the one that is hidden. A man with gray stubble on his face explains that, for the last ten years, he has been shooting what he observes through his kitchen window. He's interested in the transformation of light with each passing hour. Susan asks what his window looks out on. "A brick wall," he says, and laughter erupts.

And now it is my turn. I can tell from the silence in the room, the anticipation. When I open my eyes, the entire class is looking at me.

What am I going to share, that I am a blind person who sees? That I spend my time taking photos captured in my mind that come out blurry for most people? The pictures I end up taking are not what my eyes see. What I see has already dissolved by the time I click.

"Sorry, I didn't just wake up from a nap," I say. Weak chuckles echo against the white walls. "To concentrate, I have to close my eyes," which I do. Talking is easier if I can pretend no one is watching me.

"I have a condition called akinetopsia," I clarify, as if anyone will know what that means. "My vision is limited. . . . I don't see movement."

"Can you see light?" The voice comes from the front row.

"I can see—it's just that figures remain still for a long time. For them to move, I have to blink."

Another silence, a bit longer. "Fascinating," the cat lady says, followed by murmurs. Everyone is talking to one another now. About me.

"You're in the right class," Susan interrupts. "There's a reason we call it the art of seeing, because seeing is an art. You see more of what exists around you, if you so desire. So here we will begin to see the world through the eyes of each and every one of you."

"I once read about a man who suffered from a type of blindness that made it impossible for him to see faces," says the man with the brick wall.

"Prosopagnosia," I say. "Face blindness. We see what we are capable of seeing. That's different for all of us. That's what makes it interesting. Otherwise, we'd all take the same photographs," concludes Oscar.

The traffic is heavy when the class lets out. It'll be impossible to hail a taxi, and so I walk back the way I came, to the subway. By the time I get inside the station, I am gasping for breath. I try to relax, but as I take a deep breath I am jolted by a scent that makes my heart race so quickly I nearly lose my balance: bergamot.

I open my eyes and set off in pursuit like a wild animal. Strolling in front of me is a short, bald man talking on his cell phone. He stops to end his call and check his messages. I come to a halt behind him and try to deconstruct the essence as quickly as possible. Yes, it is the same blend I have known since childhood.

I swipe my MetroCard after him. I'm next to him. I feel I'm on the opposite side of the station, but I don't want to open my eyes. I can't lose his scent. The train is approaching. I'm standing in the middle of the platform near him. I'm lost. The man shifts, turns—is he looking at me? With every move he makes I get a hit of his bergamot. When the train enters the station, the wind tousles my hair. The smell of bergamot envelops me. What should I do? He enters the car determined, and I follow him in. I open my eyes, but I don't want to see. I hold on to the pole and come upon a warm hand. He's still there, next to me, as if he belongs to me.

"Would you like to sit down?" A girl guides me to the corner seat. I let her take me and my cane. My breathing is labored. I have to calm down. Now the man is in front of me, shielding me.

One stop and the train is full. The man inches closer to me. His leg carelessly brushes against my knee and immediately pulls away. I open my eyes and all I can see are his hands tied to the phone. I close my eyes. I don't want to see. My heart beats so loudly, I fear everyone can hear it.

How many more stops do we have to make? I sense we've already left Manhattan behind. We're in Brooklyn, I'm sure of it. One, two, three stops. I've lost count and the man is still there, in front of me, not allowing me to make the slightest move.

The train stops. The doors open. The man puts his phone away and gets ready to leave. I stand up, and people make way for me. Now I must overcome every statue by my side. The challenge is to subdue the sound and voices that begin to close in on me until I'm gasping for air.

I follow him nervously, tapping my stick on the sidewalk. In a second, I lose him, but by opening and closing my eyes several times I find him again and am able to keep him in my field of vision until he turns left onto Atlantic Avenue.

As I speed up, the last image I have is of him disappearing through a small red door with a brass bell. The high-pitched sound wave reverberates, incessantly. I start to count before opening the door. One, two, three, four . . . And my legs feel heavy, as if they want to stop me from entering.

I open my eyes. Everything is red. A dry, ancient red, so worn-out it looks like dust. Even my hands look bloodstained.

I am uncertain whether to approach and ring the bell, assuming the stranger entered a private residence, but then I realize it's a tiny store, some kind of pharmacy with a small, faded sign: Radicle Herb Shop. I go in.

It's dark inside and oddly familiar: the shelves are piled with boxes and with bags of dried herbs, and on the floor are different-colored powders in open sacks. It is like stepping back in time, to a secret sanctuary where potions are created that will transform the human body, even create eternal life. Among all the smells that assail me, I can still make out bergamot. The man is nearby. We exchange a timid, half-surprised greeting. Then the man disappears again, down some steep steps leading to the basement, the floorboards creaking underfoot as he goes. I follow him. Down below, a red-haired woman wearing a pair of thick glasses is standing behind the counter. She greets the bald man, who is apparently a regular customer. She is breathing heavily; perhaps the fragrant air is bad for her lungs. Spending each and every day in such a small, dark, enclosed space, she must have lost her sense of smell too, I imagine.

The man comes to a halt at the last shelf. Counting each step, I silently approach until I brush against him. "Sorry," he says, giving the blind girl the benefit of the doubt. I drop my stick and lean on his hand for balance. I can feel his weariness, the weight of middle age. No, he is not the one I'm looking for. My ghost is younger, energetic, and taller. An acidic smell, a mixture of smoke and sweat, permeates the air around us.

"Are you okay?" he asks, handing me my stick.

"Yes, thank you," I say.

I go closer to the shelf, which is stocked with amber bottles, all featuring handwritten, black-and-white labels. Identical to the one that toppled over me on the day of my accident.

Picking up one of the bottles, I open it and smell the fragrance. The bergamot, mixed with other ingredients, is meant to stimulate the growth of follicles on the scalp. Taking out my cell phone, I snap a photo.

I imagine my father standing in front of the same shelf, twenty years earlier. I've been here before. I can see the little girl holding her father's hand. The little girl plays between the shelves, opens small drawers, approaches the jars of dried herbs, and inhales every molecule: bergamot. The little girl tucks her hair behind her ears and continues digging through the shelves. The little girl smiles at her father. The little girl is me.

"Can I help you with anything?" asks the red-haired woman, stepping out from behind the counter. She has a true New York accent. Now she is close to me; her nicotine breath is unsettling.

I smile at her, trying to decide whether or not to purchase a bottle.

"Is it for your father? Or perhaps your boyfriend. You'd be amazed how many students come in here. Not a day over twenty. Young people today are going bald far too soon. Must be the stress."

"I'll buy one."

"You can take a sample and try it out to see if it's what you need. It's a special blend, only sold in two other pharmacies in New York."

When I open my eyes again, the woman is taking me by the hand and leading me down a narrow hallway, where the slightest misstep could knock down the many jars stacked among bags of dried herbs.

"See here? With a mix of these essences, and just the right dose, you can do anything you want. Soothe an ache, evaporate a mole, make your skin brighter, your teeth whiter. You can cure depression, allergies, even the common cold. All you need is the right combination." Then she adds, "Young people like you can digest anything, but at a certain age it's as if the filter for poison is somehow lost. Older folks, like that guy," she whispers, "need to be more careful." She turns and points to a bottle that says "Uncaria Tomentosa with Hibiscus Sabdariffa."

"A couple of drops of this can lower blood pressure. But add a few more and the descent can be uncontrollable. With these ones here, you raise it. And when I say raise it, I mean it can be explosive."

Silence. The woman lowers her head and looks at me with a half smile. "These potions and herbs can help, but if you take them too far, they can be lethal."

I already know all of this, having been around Antonia for so many years.

She picks up a tiny, unlabeled bottle tied to a small canvas bag with some dried, bristly flowers inside.

"*This* is my favorite. Without this, I wouldn't even be able to talk to you, let alone take care of those who come down to this basement. Heat water in a small saucepan, and when it reaches a rolling boil, drop in a dry star, cover the pan, and exactly three minutes later, add one drop to the water. One month into the treatment, bring it up to two drops, and the next month, three. With three, you'll feel like you entered paradise."

"Thanks," I say. "I'll just take this for now," referring to the bergamot sample. I clasp the amber bottle in my right hand and exit the store.

I take the subway back into Manhattan. My breathing finally begins to slow down when I reach Mont Cenis. I climb the stairs and pause in the corridor with my hand on the doorknob, as I did so many times when I was trying to guess if Alice was at home or not. Pressing my face against the cold surface of the door, I open my eyes. I stand there lost in thought for several minutes, disturbed by this feeling of longing. No, I don't miss feeling scared, threatened, or responsible for Alice. Thanks to her, my life is now nothing more than headline fodder.

"It's the man who I want to know about," I say out loud.

The man who smelled of bergamot is bald like my father was," I say out loud and in that instant I feel the fear has returned. "Alice's husband, no."

THIRTY-SEVEN

I have now become the sentinel of the red door. Each day, I make the trek down to Brooklyn, and I linger near it, hoping that the man I am searching for, the one with the bergamot smell, will enter the store. I'm sure I'll recognize him somehow, maybe even by his breathing.

So far, results have been minimal, though I am getting to know the neighborhood with its lovely brownstones, cafés, and boutiques.

I take the long subway ride back to Morningside Heights, but instead of going home I go to Book Culture. I head directly up to the second floor to avoid the blond cashiers. Once again, the place is full of children. I'm still trying to forget the sting of Mark no longer working here when I feel a small, soft hand take mine.

It seems like everyone wants to protect me these days. I open my eyes and look carefully at the young boy's face. He must be about seven.

"Are you afraid of dinosaurs?"

"A bit. Aren't you?"

"Of course, but I'll tell you a secret I don't want my mommy to hear." I bend down to listen, and he cups his hand around his mouth and my ear. "They don't exist. Dinosaurs don't exist, and never have."

"Wow, thanks. That makes me feel better. If they don't exist, there's nothing for us to be frightened of," I say softly.

"But do you know what I'm really afraid of? Dead people. Because they did exist, and when they died they were very angry."

"Angry? But they're dead . . ."

"That's what we think," the boy whispers, "but none of them can get used to not seeing." I hear him scamper off and feel the empty space where his warm body had been standing. Funny how children think they have the keys to the universe. I can't see, and not seeing makes me angry. Does that mean I'm dead? Or does it mean that in order to truly be alive, I must see the world like everyone else?

I wonder why I keep coming back to Book Culture. There are bookstores all over the city I could go to. Now that Mark is gone, no one selects or recommends books for me anymore; the only people who ever speak to me are curious children.

"She comes here nearly every day and never buys a book," I hear someone say as I go back downstairs. The voice, with an aroma of mandarin, wafts down from the second floor. I freeze. "She just stands there, alone in a corner with her eyes shut."

"Poor girl," replies another woman. "I don't know how she can go on living in that apartment. I'd have moved straightaway."

"But she didn't kill the man in her apartment."

"I mean the building as a whole. My grandma says it's cursed. There have been several deaths there, several suicides, over the years."

"Well, if one is on sale at half-price, I'd be the first to buy it. Can you imagine the high ceilings, the view over the park, the light you must get in those apartments? I love those prewar buildings. They don't build them like that anymore."

"I read somewhere that her mother killed her father."

"Really? I thought he had committed suicide. Did he hang himself? No! I remember now: I think he died of an overdose."

I leave the bookstore for what I know is the last time. On my way home, I stop and search through my photos. I find the image of the amber bottle I took last week, and immediately the fragrance comes back to me, as if I am holding it in my hand. I frame the photo and caption it with a single word: "bergamot." I post it.

By the time I reach Mont Cenis, likes are beginning to pop up. Someone has written the first comment: *I'm so pleased you're well!* All the rest are emojis: dark glasses, a devil's face, and lots of red, pink, and blue hearts. I scan all the comments anxiously for @star32. A sign, all I need is a sign. I am convinced the image of the bottle will be enough. I want to tell the man with the smell of bergamot that I will find him.

THIRTY-EIGHT

Oscar isn't at our weekly class tonight. When Susan projects my images from her laptop onto the interactive whiteboard I don't recognize them at first. It's as if someone else took them, not me. It's a series of rain and smoke. Drops suspended in the air, on the glass door with the park in the background, on a transparent umbrella, dissolved on the pavement, reflected in car headlights. Connor's cigarette smoke hanging in the air. The steam coming out of manholes, exhaust from subway trains and cars.

The man with the brick wall asks me if I was trying to capture what I can't see. He suggests that my next project should focus on people, the trails left behind by bodies in motion. Object guy highlights the millimetric composition of the images and asks if they were heavily edited.

At the end of class, I am the first to leave.

"I really liked your work," Susan calls out.

I find myself walking beside her to the corner of Essex and Grand, without really knowing who is following whom. We talk without looking at each other, me with my stick, tapping the sidewalk as we go along.

"You do wonders with your cell phone camera, don't you? I don't think anyone travels with those wretched digital cameras anymore. What's the point?" I wish I could see Susan's facial expressions. "Oscar is busy preparing a project right now. We're combining images from a Leica and an iPhone."

"That sounds so interesting," I say. "I admit there's a lot I don't know about photography. Proper technique, I mean. That's why I'm starting to take classes." I pause, not sure what I'm trying to say to her. "But I suppose it's also a way to try to understand life as I see it. When I open my eyes, everything I see is perfectly still. And when I take a photo with my cell phone I realize that what I saw has already disappeared. It no longer exists. Sometimes I wonder if it ever did. In my case, I really can't believe everything I see." I hope she gets the joke.

"And that's *exactly* what our class is about!" Susan says. I hear the excitement in her voice.

I stop to try to hail a cab.

"Don't even think about it—there's no chance of finding a cab here," she says. "You'd do better to just take the subway, or walk back over to Houston." She takes my hand to guide me. "I'd love to see all your photographs."

This is only the second time that anyone other than my Instagram followers has shown an interest in my photos. The first was Alice. I stop to open my bag and take out my cell phone. Should I choose what to show her? No, better let her explore. I have nothing to hide.

I can't tell which photos Susan pauses at, which ones she returns to, or which others she scarcely glances at. She's going to think I'm obsessed with Connor, following him with my phone. There are several close images of Antonia's beautiful skin. She has hardly any wrinkles. I deleted the ones of Alice.

"You have a very good eye," Susan says slowly. And then we both burst out laughing.

"Yes, I have a good eye, but what use is it to me?" Susan's smile vanishes.

"I'm so sorry."

"There's no need to be," I say.

I blink, and Susan is looking directly at me. Her eyes are big, beautiful, brown saucers. "Listen, Oscar and I would really like to do a project with you, but we were both too shy to ask."

"A project? With me? I don't think I'd be much use to you."

"He'd like to photograph you in your daily surroundings. To create new images with you that show how you sense or see things. We thought you saw everything blurred, or in black and white. But the truth is so much more interesting. We'd really like to work with you."

"Where will the project be exhibited? If it's shown anywhere outside the center, I don't want my name mentioned."

"Your name isn't necessary. We need just you and what your eyes see. And you can decide where the photos are taken. For example, here in the street, or outside the center, in your apartment, where you shop, the places you visit. We've been promised a space in a Brooklyn gallery. We were thinking I could make a video of the session, and the images would be projected at high speed—"

I interrupt her: "When do we start?"

"Whenever you like! Oscar's going to be so happy. And I already am. I'll follow you on Instagram starting right now. @BlindGirlWho Reads? Carry on taking photos, please."

I'm thrilled but then quickly feel unease in the pit of my stomach. Does Susan know who I am? Not everyone reads the *Post*, but I was named in one of the headlines that ended up on Twitter. If Susan recognizes me, surely she wouldn't have asked me to do this project with them.

"Give me your number," she says. "We can have the session this weekend. Could we start on Saturday?"

"Saturday," I say. "It's a date."

THIRTY-NINE

Oscar's arms are blue, and his neck has a violet tinge. His sick-looking hands and face seem to float independently of his body. He is wearing a small black hat jammed down on his forehead, and a white shirt done up to the top button. His black pants are so baggy they look like a skirt, and his dusty boots look like military surplus. All I can make out of Susan are her huge, chestnut-colored eyes. The rest is simply an impression: a crumpled orange dress reaching down to her ankles, a loose scarf, unkempt hair. It's the eyes, Susan's eyes, that always stand out first.

They arrived at Mont Cenis early in the afternoon, just after Antonia finished putting away the lunch dishes. The sun was still creating two rectangles on the gray living room carpet. I am waiting anxiously for Oscar to come to a standstill so that I can see him properly. Finally, he collapses onto the sofa and spreads his arms along the back. Only then can I make out the complicated tattoos that cover his arms and neck. I try to study Susan, but it's impossible: she is busy examining every corner of the room.

She probably has tattoos as well.

"I love your apartment," says Oscar.

"Would you like something to drink?" I ask nervously.

"No thanks, we're good." Susan's voice has a Southern-sounding lilt.

I go over to the French doors and stop to face the couple with my back to the daylight.

They both give off the smell of leafy woods.

"How long have you lived here?" Oscar wants to know.

"I was born here," I answer.

"Must be nice," he says. "Not to have to be a starving-artist type like us."

"Hey, let her be . . ." Susan says chidingly.

"Shall we get started?" asks Oscar, suddenly getting up. He takes off his hat and pushes back his curls.

Oscar has lots of hair, but the nape of his neck is shaven. Together with Susan, he studies the view out the window.

"Can we open the doors?" asks Susan.

"Sure, I'll do it."

As I open the French doors, the room is filled with dry air, and the light grows stronger. With his eye pressed to the viewfinder of his small black camera, Oscar approaches me cautiously, as if measuring how close he can get without invading my space. I am able to locate him by the constant click of the camera shutter.

"This okay?" he asks. "By the way, we want to use your iPhone photos as well." I feel my face light up. *Click.*

"Shall we head outside?" I ask them.

As we make our way down the corridor, Oscar runs his hand along the wall and touches the apartment's metal front door curiously. I'm not sure what he's doing, and my muscles tense.

"This building must be a hundred years old—they don't make them like this anymore," he says.

"It's from 1905, but they put in new elevators recently," I explain. "Although they kept the original wooden panels."

"All these prewar buildings are fantastic," says Susan. "You're very lucky."

I wonder where they live. In fact, I am full of questions, but unlike my new friends, I don't ask them. Out on the sidewalk, with my back to the street, I start to feel self-conscious knowing that a camera is pointed at me.

"Do you want me with the stick unfolded or closed?"

"What I want is for you not to move," says Oscar. "I'm going to count to three, and I want you to stop breathing for a few seconds. I've got the camera on a very slow speed; if you move, you grow fainter. I want the cars behind you to look blurred."

Susan is shooting video from the front stoop.

"I can't see the cars—" I start to explain.

"Don't move," Oscar says, interrupting me. "I can't see them either. I can only see you."

Motionless, I stare across the street. The bench under the oak tree is empty. I blink and see Connor, with his trail of smoke, but his cigarette has been replaced by a cell phone. I notice a gesture of contained rage. Maybe he and his girlfriend are fighting.

"Leah?" Oscar and Susan are waiting for me. I open and close my eyes again. Connor has disappeared.

Lowering the camera, Oscar takes a deep breath and dries the sweat from his forehead.

"Leah, come closer," he says. "This is how I want to portray movement."

Oscar holds out the camera and selects some photos on the small screen. I see an image of me on the sidewalk, with a hard-to-define look on my face and confused lines of color floating above the asphalt.

"Where are we going now?" I ask.

"Wherever you say. We'll follow you. You show us the way." I start to blink over and over again. I can see Oscar turning to look for Susan, who is still filming on her cell phone. She raises her thumb with a smile.

I walk toward the steps down to the park. I hold on to one of the moss-covered walls and wonder if perhaps I should have chosen a different outfit. Instead of a dress and Dad's blazer, I'm wearing black pants and one of my mother's loose white tops. I feel like another person, but Oscar is concentrating on capturing the perfect light, not on me. He ignores my poses, focusing on the angles, light, and shadows.

I'm impressed to see, or rather intuit, how Oscar and Susan communicate with each other. A tiny gesture is enough for one of them to understand what the other needs.

We leave the park and carry on walking until we reach the entrance to the majestic building on Riverside Drive and 116th Street where I've spent so many hours. I stop and look up at the top floor, at the window of Dr. Allen's apartment.

We make a detour to Le Monde, then take photos in front of Book Culture.

After the last photos, I can feel Oscar and Susan are tired. I, however, am full of energy. They have dinner plans in Brooklyn, they say. They start to put the cameras away.

"We'll walk you back," Oscar says to me.

"No need, I'm going to do some shopping." I want to sound like my life is as normal as theirs. *Their* life, I repeat silently. There are two of them. They have each other. I live alone.

Oscar and Susan both give me big hugs and then head off to the subway.

A cool spring breeze brushes past me, and I realize I'm at the building where Alice met her lawyer. I stop to look under the awning, where I expect to find a list of legal offices, but there is only a brass plate with a number on it.

"Do you need help?" the doorman says.

Something isn't right. I've had such a lovely time with Oscar and Susan, and now something is definitely not right.

"Are you looking for someone? Let me help you, miss . . ." insists the man. He has a strong Slav accent.

"What street is this?" I manage to ask him. "Have I got the wrong one?"

"What street are you looking for?"

That day we were together, Alice turned right on the corner next to Starbucks and went into the first building. I watched her turn and smile from there. I make a mental reconstruction of Alice's movements. No, I haven't made a mistake. This was the building.

"Where is the lawyer's office?"

"I'm afraid you're in the wrong place, miss. This is a residential building. There are no offices here, legal or otherwise. It's forbidden to rent the apartments to any kind of business, however much the owners would like to do so."

"It's possible they may have closed it. In this city, everything can change in a second."

"Miss, I've worked here for more than twenty years. Believe me, there's never been a lawyer's office here. In fact, in this building lawyers aren't exactly popular, or so I've heard," he says, winking.

Even more confused now, I blink toward every street corner. The rapid blur of passing cars is exhausting.

"Alice wouldn't play a trick like that on me . . ." I whisper.

"Sorry, what did you say?"

I don't reply, and the doorman goes to help a resident coming in with several shopping bags.

How am I so stupid? How did I not realize before?

"But what did she get out of lying to me?" I say out loud. There never was a lawyer. She never made that appointment. I should have come with her. I should have asked the name of the person who agreed to take on her case.

"Are you still worried about the lawyer?" The doorman has returned. "Let's see, maybe I can direct you. I'm almost certain that if you go down Amsterdam you'll find that legal office you're looking for. And if not, you'll find another one: there's lots of them on the avenue . . ."

But I am no longer listening. I am already back on Broadway with my stick.

Alice lied to me. But she can't be the only one.

I feel the sudden shock of being completely alone in the world with no one to trust, not even myself or my own senses. What else have I not seen?

FORTY

The news comes as disjointedly as everything else. First, that Antonia was brought to the hospital again. Second, that she had another heart attack. The latest voicemail message from Alejo: Antonia is in intensive care.

I should have prepared myself for the worst when she had the first heart attack. One attack usually means there will be another.

Did I give Antonia a kiss the last time I saw her? Did I hug her tight? I can't remember.

I drift like a ghost through the hospital reception area. Nobody sees me. I hear children crying, someone gasping for air, a moan, several shouts. I smell bleach and recirculated air.

The enormous coffee cup Antonia uses each morning; the flowery blue apron; the red kerchief she wears to hold back her hair; the gold chain with a delicate crucifix; her prayer cards and saints. Is that all I can remember?

If I free my mind of all thoughts, there is the possibility that whatever has been done can be undone, that Antonia will live. But my thoughts always betray me: I know there is no possible hope. I begin to count each footstep, like I used to do as a child. Six steps to the bathroom, twenty steps to the apartment door. Antonia was never very many steps away. Antonia was always there, next to me, protecting me.

If she has to die, I wish we could store Antonia's ashes in the Thomas family vault near Mom and Dad and Miles Davis. But instead, I have a vision of Alejo and me scattering them in the Hudson with the hope that they, and her saints, will cross seas and islands until they reach Cuba. It is what she wants. That is the least I can do for my dear Antonia.

Alejo emerges from her room, his face buried in his veined, dry hands.

"Oh, Leah! My Antonia has left me," I hear him say. "She has left us both."

Alejo looks diminished. His knees tremble as if they cannot bear the weight of his body. The old man begins to pray. The words come tumbling out. They have no meaning. There is no pause between them.

"She was sleeping quietly beside me. I woke up, had coffee, took her a cup. She was still lying there peacefully: I even think she was smiling. Can you believe she passed happily? God knows when exactly she went. Her body didn't even feel cold. What will become of me without her?" he asks.

God only knows, I want to say. I don't know the first thing about living. I feel a knot in my throat, but I do not cry, though it would be an appropriate time to do so. I have yet to cry for any of my dead.

Dr. Allen. I need Dr. Allen. I give Alejo a final goodbye and I call the doctor. It's late afternoon on a Wednesday, not my usual appointment time. I should come to his office now, he says, he'll be waiting for me. I must have sounded so desperate that he cleared his calendar to meet me as if it was an emergency. It is. I make my way by cab to the doctor's office.

As I near the entrance to his reception room, I hear Mrs. Allen's high-pitched shriek from their apartment next door.

"You're putting our children in danger," she's shouting, stressing each word. "Do you really think it's safe to see every one of your patients here?"

"Ann, you know very well it was an accident, done in absolute self-defense. Leah has been with me for years. Her neurological condition, combined with a serious emotional disorder, has made it nearly impossible for her to live a normal life. She's frustrated and desperately lonely. I can't deny there is some violence in her past, but before Alice and her abusive husband came along, it had been ten years since her last episode."

I stand there, motionless.

"Richard, that girl killed someone. In cold blood! How can you trust her?"

I can feel the energy drain out of me. My knees buckle, and I am filled with an immense sadness. Perhaps I should leave and never return. Almost a year has passed since Michael Turner's death, and the world still sees me as a threat. Am I? There have been times I've thought I was the one in danger, until I decided not to be. But is fear a choice? Either you're in danger, or you're not. I don't know what to think anymore.

All at once, the sound of a door slamming. I pray to Antonia's spirits that Mrs. Allen will not come out into the waiting room and find me listening.

I walk into the consulting room, and, just as I do, I hear her leave through another door.

Dr. Allen is slumped in his chair, staring down at his notebook, pen at the ready. From the doorway, I can hear his irregular breathing; with each breath, the doctor's body seems to swell up, like that of an animal that breathes through its skin.

"I'm so sorry. I heard what your wife was saying about me. I can leave if you want me to."

"No, of course not. Sit, sit."

"Antonia's dead."

"I'm so sorry to hear about Antonia. I know how important she was to you." He doesn't dare to look at me. I don't say anything.

"I remember that when you were a little girl your mother used to say that God had put you on this earth to see what others couldn't. You're not blind, Leah."

No, but there's a lot I can't see. Mostly because everyone's lied to me about who and what I am, I want to say. Still, I remain silent.

"I have to say I'm worried about you living on your own." The doctor stands up and comes to me.

Every time he does this, I know he is coming to examine my eyes. They are misty, on the verge of tears.

Warm fingers. I can feel every line of his fingerprints from the thumb, index, and middle finger of his right hand. He opens my eye, as if he wants to see my insides, beyond the iris, the pupil, as if he wants to read my thoughts.

"You know you can always count on me. We should get a scan soon. When was the last time you had a checkup?"

The doctor goes to his computer, searches in silence. I refuse to undergo another MRI that will get me nowhere.

"Two years ago," I say.

"I'd like to see your photographs one of these days, your stories too. It wouldn't be a bad idea for you to start printing them out for me."

I want to hug him for pretending, for my sake, that life is that easy. As if by my showing him these things, my life will take another turn. But that's ridiculous. In the last year, each member of my family, or what I called my family, has left me. How can I go on now? Is Dr. Allen next?

"I've started a new life," I say.

"I'm glad to hear it." Dr. Allen doesn't seem convinced.

"I have new friends," I insist.

I remain stranded in the middle of the room, in silence, as if I were one of my images.

Suddenly, I've forgotten where I am.

"Leah!" He is shouting and shaking me, and I get the sense that he has been for some time.

"You need help at home." Dr. Allen's voice is now deep, confident. "You can't be alone. You can't take care of yourself."

"Now you want to lock me up?" I scream and lunge toward the mound of books stacked next to the armchair. I throw them in the air. Yes, I want to scream, rush over to him, and throw him out the window. Leave my eyes open, wide open, without blinking. I look for my file, open it, and, one by one, tear the pages of my story in half. I move to the wall behind the desk, take down one of his framed diplomas, and hurl it against the floor.

Dr. Allen's wife opens the door and screams when she sees me.

"You need to go, Leah," says the doctor, so calmly it's exasperating.

The door remains open for me. The wife takes shelter in a corner as if I am going to attack her. She's covering her face with her hands.

I leave and slam the door. The echo of the bang follows me to the elevator. The nosy neighbor is staring at me through a crack in his door.

FORTY-ONE

Time has lost all meaning. I haven't looked at my phone for days. Or maybe it's been weeks, I'm not sure. I have barely eaten, barely gotten up out of bed. I have not read, taken photos, or written any stories. I am alone and in complete darkness. The look of horror on Mrs. Allen's face told me everything that eighteen years of living under her husband's care had not: *this* is my destiny.

I can't remember the last time I spoke to anyone. Connor has knocked on my door three separate times. Twice I didn't answer. The third time I spoke to him through the door, telling him that I was okay. I know he is keeping watch over me, warding off the social workers, now that I no longer go to the appointments with Dr. Allen. I know that Connor will not hesitate to call the authorities if it looks like I have gone missing or am harming myself.

The family next door must be walking around on their tiptoes, they are so quiet. Though I do hear the child run from one corner of the apartment to the other every so often. They have a cat that doesn't meow but scratches the baseboards of the walls. I talk to it sometimes. Cats feel and see more than you think.

I hear pings from my phone now and again, but I ignore them. Until one day I get a call. Susan.

Her voice is cracked. She sounds nervous. She didn't expect me to answer and isn't sure how to begin the conversation. Yes, I'm fine. I don't have the energy to apologize for missing class. Susan sounds cautious, measuring every word like she's trying not to hurt me or sound invasive.

"Are you free on Saturday?" she asks.

Of course I am. "Is that when you're showing the exhibit?"

"Oh, no. The space won't be ready for another week. But we wanted to invite you to the gallery. A friend of ours has a show, and they're taking it down next week. We'd like to take you so that you can tell us what you think of the space. It's called the Invisible Dog. Shall we meet around eight? I'll send you the address."

"There are no accidents. Everything that happens in this life, we cause, we create," I hear Antonia tell me.

I am the architect of everything that has befallen me. I'm not sure what my next move will be. It seems I am creating a labyrinth with no idea where it will lead, or what I will find along the way. By now I've lost all faith in myself; nothing I've ever done has been good or brought me any happiness.

But then it occurs to me that this time might be different. I enrolled in a class with strangers. I allowed myself to be photographed. I permitted two strangers to tell their version of my story, which might be better than anything I might have ever come up with on my own.

It's almost dawn and I haven't been able to sleep. A soft rain comes and goes outside. The raindrops drip slowly onto the metal covering of the air-conditioning unit outside my room. I count them one by one.

On Saturday afternoon, I take a long, hot bath, and then get ready. I apply red lipstick and eyeliner, like my mother taught me. In front of the mirror, I struggle to ward off all the presentiments overwhelming me. What am I hoping to find tonight? Why did I agree to go somewhere that in my mind is yet another black hole? I am sure this is another world I have willed into existence, just like the mystery of the daguerreotype, the bergamot man. Nothing around me exists anyway; I am clearly living in a world that my own mind has imagined.

I pull on a pair of black leggings and a loose, long-sleeved black blouse. Riding boots that reach my knees. At first I don't recognize myself. Then I see Alice. Or at least, the Alice I once thought I knew. I reach back and am surprised by the feel of my exposed neck.

My new pixie cut suits me.

The next time I open my eyes, a taxi is waiting for me. The next time, we are going over a bridge. Finally, we are outside the entrance to the Invisible Dog. All of this happens in the blink of an eye. Somehow, it's all familiar.

"Leah!" An excited shout erupts from behind me. Susan. "We thought you weren't coming! What do you think of the place?"

Now I feel like I've gotten my life back: I'm independent; I have friends.

I would be exaggerating if I said I could actually see the space, but I am able to get a sense of it: it is a huge, infinite black dot. I can't make out the roof or the walls, and there is a constant throbbing noise echoing in the emptiness. The gallery is filled with light, or rather beams of light that merge and melt into one another. The current exhibit consists of videos and light displays. Everything is whirling around me like a carousel that is out of control and can't be stopped. The smells of alcohol, mint, and sugary essences mingle with traces of dry yeast, the tanned leather of bags, with sweat and pores oozing nicotine, musk-based perfumes, rose, and citrus.

"What do you make of it?" Oscar shouts in my ear. "It's a friend of ours showing his work. And after him, it'll be our turn!"

"Where will the photographs be shown?" I ask.

"Our idea is that they should float, hang from the ceiling as if they are moving. Susan's videos will be projected onto the walls, combined with your photos of rain and smoke. Can you see it? I mean . . . can you imagine how it might look?"

Oscar takes my hand and leads me toward another room. There

is a line to enter; it's protected by a huge wooden door with iron bars. Whenever the security guard opens the door to let someone exit, gray fog seeps out. Based on the sounds, the room is completely packed: when ten people depart, only two are allowed in.

"Don't worry," Susan says. "It's dark inside." She can tell I'm nervous.

Finally, the door opens slowly in front of us, and we edge our way in. "I can't see a thing," Oscar says. I smile at the irony.

I begin to make out the vertical lines of the room. A beam of light shoots across the empty air, landing on bodies that are stepping aside to let me pass by. I feel like everyone is looking at me, until Oscar and Susan rescue me from the glare, guiding me past obstacles to the far end of the room.

I take a whiff of the air around me, and in that instant I know why I am here.

"You all right, Leah?" Susan asks, taking me by the arm. "You're trembling."

"Would you like to leave?" asks Oscar. "I can understand, this place is too dark."

"I think I recognized someone." I smile so as to allay their concern.

"In this darkness? No way," Susan says.

"I think I'm going to leave and go home. But don't worry; I'm fine."

"We'll go with you to find a taxi," Oscar offers.

"There's no need. Really, I'm fine. Let's talk tomorrow. Don't worry, I'll call for an Uber when I get outside. I always get around better in the dark anyway."

I make my way back through the crowd, following the scent of bergamot.

FORTY-TWO

My fingers are twitching uncontrollably; I can barely keep hold of my white stick. I come to a stop in the middle of the photo gallery, behind a man with his back to me. I study his white shirt with the sleeves rolled up, the sweat on the nape of his neck. In an instant, he feels familiar, as if I know him. The fear has returned. The unmistakable scent of bergamot is in the air, but it isn't concentrated on a single person. I feel a desperate urge to get in front of him and bring my nose as close as I can to his neck, but just at that moment someone passes between us and pushes me away from him.

I'm lost. When I blink, the man has vanished, but a few seconds later I make him out at the exit. I follow him, bumping into couples trying to get their bearings in the darkness. I know my friends' eyes are on me—out of concern, they might try to follow me—but the shadowy gloom is a perfect shield.

Obsessed by the smell, I hurry after it, and realize I am defenseless outside the gallery. Around me, men are smoking, leaning against the wall; a girl is waiting for a car; a couple is hurling insults at each other. I see the man turn the corner a few yards in front of me. I blink repeatedly so as not to lose him. What I wouldn't give to see his face, I tell myself; maybe I can catch up to him and ask him the time or for directions. But that makes no sense: he would recognize me and leave me stranded on the sidewalk. *Why are you following me? What do you want from me? Isn't one dead man enough for you?*

Still, I follow him at a distance, my eyes closed. From time to time I blink, to store the images in my memory. I study him, taking in his silhouette.

I know I have taken my obsession too far. I can hear Antonia's voice scolding me ("Don't go looking for trouble, my love") and the warnings Dr. Allen has given me ("You have many special gifts, Leah, but very few people see the world as you do"). I notice that the man has taken his cell phone out of his pocket and slowed down. I follow him for one, two, three blocks, until I no longer know where I am. I have no idea how to get back to the gallery, and nobody will hear me if I cry out in the deserted street. It is probably close to midnight, and here I am, alone and sightless, following the man who has tormented me for months. Or has he? Nothing is completely real to me anymore. There is no way to confirm he is the one until I come face-to-face with him and can touch him. Just a single brush against him would be enough. Simply coming into contact with him would serve as proof.

The man comes to a halt in front of a brownstone at the end of the street. He puts away his phone and takes out a set of keys. Hesitant, with sweaty palms, I realize I'm not ready for this. What if it isn't him? As the seconds tick by, I become increasingly terrified and the smell of bergamot intensifies.

But it is already too late; I can't run away. I take another step and pause in midair before taking the next one. I am shivering. I am losing control of my body and feel a piercing cold. My head is spinning, and I am so close to him that he must see me.

First image: the man descending the brownstone steps to garden level. Second image: him pushing the key into the lock. Third image: his face—shocked, concerned, and beautiful, just as I had imagined—staring back at mine.

I know I am about to collapse. Scarcely breathing, mute and terrified, I lose my balance and drop my white stick. In a desperate lunge, I cling to the man's arm.

My nostrils dilate to take in as much air as possible. I stare straight at him again and collapse.

It is him. I knew it.

FORTY-THREE

I wake up startled, with traces of bergamot jabbing at my throat. Still in darkness, I feel as if I'm floating on an unsteady cloud. When I try to shift position, I'm shaken by a sudden pain in my knees. Am I bleeding? I want to feel my body to search for wounds, but I'm unable to. Am I tied up? I move my arms and legs to check. No, I'm not tied up.

I think perhaps I have been shut inside a dark basement. How long have I been here? Hours, days? I try to understand how I could have ended up here. I had followed the man who had been stalking me ever since the first night I slept in my mother's bedroom. So this must be my punishment. "Those who seek shall find," I can hear Antonia say. But what, or who, did I want to find? Why had I followed him in the first place?

I hear a distant voice, little more than a murmur. Whoever it is doesn't want me to hear. If I open my eyes and concentrate, I could make out what is being said, even if it's only disjointed, meaningless phrases. My head hurts, and I feel feverish. *Wake up!* I tell myself. I begin to count: one, two, three . . . I need help to recover. Yes, there is someone outside—I can hear him better now. The voice is familiar. It is a man, alone, and he seems to be answering questions. I have to get up, to see where the voice is coming from, ask for help, cry out, escape. I open my eyes, convinced I must be hallucinating.

"What do you want me to do?" A pause. "She's asleep . . ." A longer pause. "I don't think she's woken up yet . . ."

The tone of that voice: I know that voice.

The door at the opposite end of the room opens. It must lead out to a garden or yard.

Yes, it is an interior yard. I'm not in a basement.

"I can't tell her to leave at this time of night . . . she looks so helpless."

So it is still night; that means I have not been here long. But why does my entire body ache? I must have fallen hard when I passed out. My God, what have I done? How do I get out of here?

I don't see the man reenter the room but hear the floorboards creak. I blink and see him near the door, but realize this must be an earlier image, because I can feel that the warmth the stranger's body gives off is much closer. The smell of bergamot is intense. The man's voice and hazy outline reach me:

"Are you okay?"

I blink once, twice. I can't believe who is standing before me.

I fill my lungs with air and squeeze my eyes shut, and a strange feeling of relief washes over me. I do not respond.

Mark. I blink and see his face leaning over me, so close that I can make out the pores between his eyebrows, which are drawn together, the stubble on his chin, the razor burn at the corners of his mouth, his stale breath.

Mark . . . Where did he leave his hat? And his glasses and beard?

I stir, sigh, and sit up on the sofa. I straighten the cushions and cover myself with the blanket, as if I have no clothes on. I do not dare look directly at him, but stare into space, like a blind person. Day is dawning. I feel ashamed.

He smiles awkwardly and sits on the sofa beside me. He hands me my stick, as if I might need it to sit up, as if I can't see him. Playing along, I take it in both hands.

"Thanks," I say, looking directly at him for the first time. His eyes are a dull grayish green, as if they hold the night inside them.

There is an uncomfortable silence, then he smiles at me again.

"I'm so sorry, Mark," I say, and look down.

"You scared me, Leah," he says eventually. "But I realized you had only fainted. I didn't know if I should call 911 for help, but in the end, I called a friend, just to see what they thought I should do."

A friend, yes, a friend. I bow my head, embarrassed. He can't be the man I'd thought he was, the man who broke into my apartment. He is my Mark from Book Culture. How is it that I never noticed his bergamot scent before? I know. When I am nervous, when I am surrounded by people, when I want to isolate myself, I block my strongest sense. It is the barrier I always build.

Mark strokes his smooth, shaved head and smiles.

"Don't worry," he says. "I imagine you were lost. This isn't a very good neighborhood to be out on your own at night."

"I was looking for the subway." I hope I sound convincing.

"Well, you were heading in the wrong direction. And you're pretty far from home."

"I came out of the gallery. My friends are going to have an exhibit there," I say.

"Really? You were in the Invisible Dog? What a coincidence. I went because it was the show's last day. I was meaning to go sooner but I've been busy with work."

"Coincidences don't exist," I hear Antonia's voice.

"What happened with Book Culture?"

"Oh." He sounds guilty, like he feels bad for having left me. "No . . . well, I finished school. I work for a website and I'm an actor . . ."

"Are you in a play?"

"Not at the moment."

I notice some black-and-white photographs on the bookshelves, a poster with red lettering: *They Shoot Horses, Don't They?* In the photographs, he has thick, curly hair.

"Would you like something to drink? Water? Coffee?"

I refuse with a slow wave of my hand, but he stands up anyway and leaves the room. Left to my own devices, I look around. Stacks of newspapers, theater programs, books everywhere, photos strewn all over the floor. The walls are lined with bookshelves, except for one: it is plastered with photographs, drawings, posters. A real home, I think. This is how normal people live. I'm the only one who feels protected by emptiness.

I need a central point in order to understand the layout of the room and get my bearings. Drowsy, I shake my head and realize that my fainting spell and fall are the reason I feel so befuddled; I also realize that I am not, and never have been, afraid of this man. All of this bewilders me: I ought to feel scared. Fear is like fever, nature's perfect form of defense.

Mark brings me a glass of water and I take it. I pretend to drink, then stand up. "I have to go," I say. On my feet, leaning on the white stick, I look for a way out. "May I use your bathroom?"

He holds out his hand and guides me to a door. I turn my back on him and slowly close it. Switching on the light, I study myself in the mirror of the small medicine cabinet. My skin appears yellow in its dim glow. Dark shadows extend from underneath my eyes and across my cheeks. The room is tiny, everything within reach. I open the medicine cabinet, and the smell of bergamot floods the space. There sits an amber bottle. The same amber bottle of my father's.

I take out my phone and order an Uber. I want to run away. I can hear Mark's breathing on the other side of the door. He is either worried I will faint again, or he is spying on me.

I use my stick to open the door and boldly cross the living room.

"Shall I call you a car?"

I exhale with relief. "I've already ordered an Uber, thanks. It should be here in three minutes." I walk to the front door. He opens it for me.

"I don't know how to thank you," I hear myself say. "You must let me take you to dinner."

"I work in the evenings, but maybe next Saturday . . ." He breaks off, disappears inside, and returns with a folded piece of paper. He hands it to me with a smile. "Here's my phone number. Thanks for the invitation. Call me if you really mean it."

It sounds like an order. I am unable to make out his gestures or the expression on his face. He is constantly on the move.

I hear a car stop in front of us. "Leah?" the Uber driver asks.

I hasten into the car, as if to cut short the farewell.

"Goodbye," I say, closing the car door.

I unfold the piece of paper. He has written his name and number in bright blue ink.

FORTY-FOUR

Every night that week I am tempted to call him. I unfold and fold the piece of paper time and again; I read it so many times I know his number by heart. And every night I dream of him. On Saturday afternoon, I finally phone him.

"Hi there, it's Leah. Do you remember me?"

"You're the only Leah I know. Are you feeling better?"

I want to say that I wasn't ever sick. I recall his tone of voice, his calm eyes, his reassuring gestures. And his smell. The smell that has always been with me.

"Yes, thanks. I thought we could go to my friends' show together tonight," I say straight-out, and immediately regret it: I don't want to sound too eager. "But before that we could have dinner. I owe you one."

"You owe me nothing. But yes, let's meet for dinner first, then the exhibit. Do you like Thai? Let's go to Lemongrass."

"Great."

"Seven o'clock?"

"Seven it is," I say, as if I ask strangers out all the time. But Mark is not a stranger to me. Mark is mine.

I sink into a warm bath covered in foam, and let my imagination run away with me. I have to forget about the bergamot, to lose my fear. The man with the bergamot scent doesn't have a face; Mark does.

The water comes up to my cheeks, and for a few minutes I float, daydreaming. I imagine myself roaming the city with Mark, and then sitting beneath a leafy tree, hand in hand. My head leaning on his shoulder, my stick nowhere to be found. From now on I could live with my eyes closed; I feel secure. I place my hand gently on my pelvis and move downward, stroking. He smiled at me in a way that made me tremble. I am about to cry out but at that moment the water covers my face and I sit upright, gasping for breath. I have to hurry; it will take me at least an hour to cross Manhattan and reach Brooklyn.

I put on a pair of jeans and a baggy sweater, then comb my straight hair and find a pair of my mother's earrings. I pose in front of the mirror. *Mark, Mark, Mark*, I repeat to myself as I try to find the smile I like best.

When I get out of the Uber in Brooklyn, he is waiting for me in front of his building, hands in his pockets. It looks as if he is wearing the same clothes he had on a week earlier: black pants and a T-shirt, except that now he also has on an olive-green jacket. He hugs me.

I can feel Mark's hand touching my back, almost caressing me. Is this pity or a sign of affection?

We begin to walk, and I wonder whether to get out my stick, but instead close my eyes and take his arm. I have a guide now; there is no reason for me to worry about any obstacles, the static images, or sounds coming from nowhere.

When I open my eyes again, I am sitting at a table in the corner of a packed restaurant. Voices mingle with the sounds of cutlery and glasses. I am thrown off by the smell of grilled fish, fried onion, and yeast. I discover I am drinking red wine, but can't remember having ordered it. I need to stop paying attention to all that is going on around me: The girl sitting behind me, complaining to her friend about the boyfriend who just left her. Another one in despair because her parents are no longer helping with rent. The bored couple at the next table, staring at their phones.

"Everything okay? This place is a tad noisy."

The lady opposite has sent back her food several times. "It's undercooked, it's overcooked, it's too spicy." The waiter is complaining behind the swing door to the kitchen. "Calm down, calm down," his colleagues are telling him, chortling with laughter. "I'll take care of it," the girl working the bar offers. "That woman is just trying to get a free meal."

"Leah?"

"Who's going to serve the blind girl? You or me?" I hear.

Mark takes my hand and strokes it to get my attention.

"I'm sorry, it takes me a while to get used to a new environment."

"I understand. If you don't like it, we don't have to stay."

"No, I'm fine, it's just that—"

"Would you like me to read the menu for you?" he says, ready to recommend his favorite dishes.

"I doubt there's enough light in here for you to read it," I tell him. "I can though. In fact, this semidarkness is better for me."

The waiter arrives, and I order first.

"The salmon salad."

"The same for me," says Mark, without paying much attention to the waiter. Silence. Mark doesn't dare look me in the eye.

"I've been thinking about you all week, but you didn't leave me your phone number. I was beginning to think you wouldn't call me."

"The fact is, I hesitated a long time before calling you. I couldn't imagine what you thought of me, showing up behind you like that."

"Well, I have to confess it's not every day that a beautiful woman faints at your feet . . . and right outside your front door!"

"It had been a long day, I got lost, and I was frightened. I'm sorry." A beautiful woman: I flush at the thought.

"No need to be ashamed. Thanks to that, I found you."

He found me. He's trying to tell me he's been looking for me.

Mark gives off a different fragrance. The smell of bergamot has disappeared completely. I am not afraid.

"Were you born with the problem?" he asks as if he doesn't know me, as if we've never spoken, and I play along.

I shake my head vigorously.

"So you used to be able . . . I've always wanted to understand how you see." The waiter arrives with our salads. "Sorry for all the questions. I just want to know you better now."

"When I was little, I could see perfectly," I say between bites. "Then I had an accident. A glass shelf fell on top of me."

"It must have been very tough for you."

"It was, and for my parents too. But they're no longer with us. I live on my own," I say. Laying a hand on my stomach, I smile shyly. "That was delicious."

As Mark asks for the bill, his phone starts to vibrate.

"Excuse me a second. I have to take this call," he says apologetically, getting to his feet and walking quickly away, out of my field of vision.

However much I blink, there is always somebody coming into the restaurant at that moment, or a waiter standing close to me holding aloft a loaded tray. The intense smell of tomato sauce with basil is fading, but the waiter is still there, like a barrier separating me from Mark. Why was I overcome with fear when he moved away from me? He received a call that couldn't wait. He could have answered it at the table but avoided doing so. Why? What could it mean?

Stop it, I chide myself. I need to enjoy myself, let all of these suspicions and bad feelings go.

"Shall we?" His voice is close to me. "I've taken care of the bill, so we can leave, unless you'd like something else."

"Oh, but I invited you! You shouldn't have."

"Come on, or we'll be late for the gallery."

Arm in arm once again, we emerge out onto the street.

FORTY-FIVE

Mark bumps fists with the doorman, who opens the gallery door for us. A group of hipsters is outside, anxious to be let in. I see a black poster divided in two by horizontal orange stripes. At the top, the title of the exhibit: "The Silence in Her Eyes." Underneath, the names of the artists: "Oscar Green and Susan Nelson."

The gallery is packed with people. Mark escorts me to a quiet spot, and when I open my eyes I am facing a huge black-and-white projection of my face, my eyes slowly opening and closing. I wasn't expecting the images to be this size, to be featured so prominently in the show. I feel embarrassed. I don't want Mark thinking I am showing off. As the image dissolves, a new one appears, creating an endless sequence. Now I am standing in front of Mont Cenis. Color gradually seeps into the photo, with my eyes turning an intense blue.

"What do you think?" I hear Susan ask at my shoulder.

"We haven't slept, we've been so busy putting it all together," adds Oscar, smiling. I don't know what to say.

"I never imagined the images would be so big. I was expecting small photographs in frames on the walls . . ."

"Oh no, you should never have expected anything so boring from us, Leah!" says Oscar, laughing. "But do you like them?"

"Of course I do; I love them!"

"How do you two know each other?" asks Susan, curious to see me on Mark's arm.

"I met him last Saturday. Well, actually, we first met at Book Culture." I turn to Mark.

Mark can't stop moving. I can't see his expression, what he's thinking. His face is a blur.

This is their territory, I think to myself. I'm the impostor here. My eyes are imprinted, arrested, on huge cardboards. The word *silence* repeats between my eyes. Suddenly I feel that these are not my eyes.

Mark sees I am nervous and puts his arm around my shoulders. He whispers discreetly, "We can leave whenever you like. There are too many people here. I know you hate crowds, and I'm beginning to feel the same way."

"Why don't we go to your place?" I pluck up the courage to ask, then add, to hide my embarrassment: "If you want to, that is."

I can't make out the reaction on Mark's face, but a few seconds later he takes me by the hand and we leave the gallery without saying goodbye to anyone. Behind us the strobe lights are crisscrossing the walls. Recurring flashes show my face projected in the air. At times, my eyes go from a bright, empty white to encroaching darkness.

The gallery was so full that the doors were closed, and a line of people hoping to enter snakes around the corner of the street. Mark and I are the only ones leaving. We walk slowly along the dark streets, unsure of what to say. I consider calling an Uber; everything is happening so fast. I tell myself that I have always felt safe with Mark. I'm coming to understand that that other man, the one who pursued me in the darkness of my bedroom, was just a figment of my imagination. Mark is not my enemy: I have been waiting for him all my life. As I nestle my hand in his, I even doubt whether Alice and Michael ever really existed. The bergamot smell has vanished.

"The thing is, I feel so good being around you," he says.

"Me too."

"It's as though I can't see clearly either, and walking along beside you aimlessly, not knowing where we are headed, is totally okay. I'm exactly where I want to be," he says.

As we approach his building, my heart begins to pound. I inhale nervously, trying to silence it. I can sense that Mark's heart is also racing.

As we walk down the stairs to open the door, he smiles and leans over me.

"Don't tell me you're going to faint again," he jokes gently. "Don't worry, I'm nervous too."

Taking me by the hand once more, he leads me across the threshold in darkness. Then we are standing silently in the middle of the living room. I breathe in the smell of dried ink, soot, burnt logs. I register and process them, but immediately forget them when I sense the warmth coming from Mark's body. We are so close that I can tell he is holding his breath, and then I feel the rough contact of his unshaven cheek with my smooth one. I let him embrace me, and I return his embrace.

My legs begin to buckle, but I am no longer afraid I might faint. He will hold me up.

The first kiss is gentle, and besides, it isn't my first one: I have lived all the kisses I've read about in my books, other people's caresses and embraces. At first our lips feel dry, but it is a pleasurable sensation. As they moisten, I gradually let myself go. This kiss, I feel, will determine my future.

Now we are naked. No more masks. This is me. A sea of sharp needles begins to enter my every pore. A new kind of pain makes me cry out. The tingling in my spine is ecstasy. Enveloped in a silent cry that isolates me, I allow myself to be intoxicated by the sweetish smell of saliva. My body is melting into that of a man I vaguely know, someone I watched silently and imagined to be my friend, someone who has disturbed my dreams. Now Mark is going to be my friend, my true friend. I feel my silent eyes filled with the watery blue of tears.

FORTY-SIX

I am going to fall in love with this man. With him I am going to be happy, and with him I will have a child, I keep repeating in order not to forget. Yes, a single night with Mark has been enough to confirm it.

Now he has a face, a completely different one, nothing like the one in my fantasies or in the daily visits to Book Culture. That man hiding beneath a hat and a dark beard now has a profile. I have left the rest, like that terrible nightmare bergamot smell, far behind me.

I imagine him as a child, with his parents, jumping in the rain. I envision him performing onstage, gazing out to the audience with his beautiful, inquisitive eyes.

I read each and every one of Mark's text messages over and over, though I would prefer to hear his voice, to receive a phone call. The first messages only talk about the exhibit, the images of a girl lost in the lights of the city. As the days go by, they end with more personal phrases: *I'm dying for Saturday to come, I can't stop thinking about you, I miss you.*

Every message leaves me breathless.

When Saturday finally does come, I dress very carefully and hail a taxi headed for Brooklyn. Once I arrive, I knock twice and open the door, as Mark instructed me to. He would be waiting for me, he said. There was no need for us to go out—we didn't have to eat or drink; he simply wanted to be with me, and the sooner the better, he wrote. As soon as I enter, I recognize the feeling of peace. There is no noise in his apartment; there are no sounds of nearby footsteps or fragments of other people's conversations. It is as if the neighbors have gone away and left us the whole block to ourselves, as if the ambulances and firemen are on strike for the day.

Mark is lying on the sofa with a pillow over his face. On the table I see glasses and a bottle of wine. The books that were strewn every-where before, the piles of newspapers and empty beer cans, have all vanished. Nor are there any clothes thrown into corners, or shoes under the armchairs. The only light comes from a lamp by the door that opens out to the garden. Mark is either asleep or pretending to be. I cross the room toward him. I wonder what would be the best way to wake him, and begin to tremble when I hear a dull thud. Something in the room has fallen, or perhaps . . . I blink and see a book on the floor at the foot of the bed. Fear attracted fear.

"What's going on?" asks Mark, sitting up with a start and taking me by the hands.

"Have you been here long?"

I wish he hadn't woken up like this. I had hoped to wake him with the same type of kiss he had given me last Saturday. I want to slowly take his clothes off and explore his body, discover every shadow.

"I spent the day working hard so the apartment would look better for you," he says with a smile, still half asleep.

I drop my bag on the sofa. Within seconds, he is devouring me. My eyes shut, I feel Mark's lips moving over my breasts, my stomach, my legs, while he holds my body tight, as though to prevent me from escaping.

Afterward, we both lie looking up at the ceiling in silence. Mark turns to me and takes hold of my right hand and squeezes it.

He begins telling me about the theater, his studies, his job at the website.

"I work from Monday to Friday at a digital company, and some weekends in the theater. But I'm tired of the actor's life."

"My father was an actor too." I can't remember whether I told him that before or just imagined that I told him.

"Was he successful?"

"He was very handsome, very observant, and very charming. My mom said that just one look and you wanted to know everything about him. When he spoke, everyone had to listen. He won you over with his words. I'd fall asleep with the stories and characters he made up. Now I can't even remember his voice. He died of an overdose before he ever found real success."

In the shutter image I had from a few seconds before, Mark was smiling. When I blink again, I see his lips are pursed. I can't see his eyes.

FORTY-SEVEN

The sound of the door slamming, walls shaking, heavy, determined footsteps. I look at the clock. It is two in the morning, and I am in my apartment alone. Without turning the lights on, I step out of my bedroom and into the living room. Yet again I can sense the intruding steps behind me, almost upon me; this time though I am ready to confront him, whoever he might be, even if he is no more than something I created in my mind. I have to destroy my ghosts as well. There is no way I was going to remain hidden under my blanket, smelling the odor of a stranger, feeling the pressure of a hand suffocating me.

The man catches me by the hair and drags me farther back into the bedroom. I don't let out so much as a groan: nothing can hurt me. I want to see my enemy's face once and for all. Wearing a dark leather glove, the hand covers my mouth to prevent me from crying out. Rather than taking in oxygen to survive, my nose is focused on recognizing my attacker, whose face is covered by a balaclava. Not far from me, I can hear more footsteps: these are slow and dainty. I make out a woman standing barefoot in the doorway, wearing a red dress. I keep my eyes wide open while I am in the man's grip. His breath is dense, like an old person's.

The woman raises a knife in her right hand.

Alice, I want to say, *forgive me*, though I am not sure why I am asking for forgiveness. *Alice*, I repeat silently. I open and close my eyes, and now see Alice standing beside me, weeping, the knife down by my side. I could stretch out my fingers without the man in the balaclava seeing me, and in a flash take the knife and plunge it into his neck. It is the very opportunity I have been waiting for all these months. The metal blade would kill him, and I would be free of him at last. Twenty-four blows, and he would be dead.

Now I am looking at the dead man and Alice from on high. Without blinking, I stab at Alice's neck, letting out a long, high-pitched scream.

Eyes open, now I am in my bed, in my apartment without Mark. I am under my white comforter, covered in sweat, in utter darkness. My nightmares have returned and, with them, the smell of bergamot.

Before I drifted off to sleep, Mark and I had been texting back and forth; his question is still floating in the air. Until now, he has not suggested we see each more than once a week. But this Friday, he did.

Come stay with me?, I read once more.

I blink, and Mark is beside me. I had left my apartment with all its nightmares and gone to Brooklyn without giving it a thought, with no plan. I enter his apartment fearlessly, as if I have always lived there. Certain that I have driven away forever the shadows that had been such a torment.

"I already know your freckles by heart, and yet every day I discover a new one. Now all the new ones are mine," says Mark, tracing a line of them along my nose and then my cheeks, as if he wants to spread them all over my face. I keep my eyes closed, enchanted by all these new sensations I am not sure how to react to, overwhelmed by the voice whispering in my ear things I have never heard before. Tears of joy spring up in my eyes, and I don't want him to see me crying.

FORTY-EIGHT

The following Saturday, Mark is waiting for me out on the sidewalk. He has learned: he stands perfectly still so that I have no problem making him out.

"Mark," I say.

"I can't go on waiting for weekends to arrive!" he says, giving me a kiss. "It's too long."

"I know, for me too. What shall we do? I'll do whatever you say."

We enter the apartment arm in arm. As I step inside, the world that I usually navigate in darkness is suddenly lit up.

"Mark, I want to sell my apartment," I blurt out. "Let's find a house for the two of us."

"Is that what you really want?" he replies. He sounds hesitant.

"What do you want?"

"To live with you, of course."

"We could live in one half of the apartment and open a studio in the other half, or any other project you have. Maybe you could start acting again, who knows?"

Mark pulls me to him and embraces me. He whispers softly in my ear:

"There's plenty of time for that. What I want right now is for you to come here and stay with me properly. I can't bear having you leave when the weekend is over."

Mark is unaware of the effect his words have. I am saying good-bye to everything. My childhood home, Morningside Park, a life-time of memories, even my akinetopsia. What do I need movement for now? I want everything, including time, to come to a stop.

In bed, I undress him slowly. Entering into the game, he lets me do so. Now I have my eyes open, blinking, taking him in. This is the first time I have seen him naked, that I have him in front of me with my eyes open. Little by little, Mark's hands merge with his face; when they reach my stomach, his lips are still within reach. I think of it as a single caress. A lengthy, everlasting caress.

We have been spending our nights in bed, laptop between us, checking real estate websites. We find a listing for a house in Dobbs Ferry, a quaint town north of the city. It shows a beautifully restored colonial, built of stone and wood, with a charming garden. Mark has dreamed of a place overlooking the river, a place where he could have friends over, and I could finish the novel I've been trying to write, *A Normal Girl*. But the truth is I haven't written a word since I left the hospital.

The next weekend, Mark rents a red car. We are driving away from the city, leaving the island behind. Every now and then he reaches over and takes my hand.

We are heading north. I am no longer frightened by the road. Window down, the fresh air calms me.

We reach Cricket Lane at noon. The real estate agent has not yet arrived. Mark walks up to the house and peeks inside the windows.

"It's huge," he says.

I lean against the door and it opens. We both smile.

"Should we go inside?" he asks.

Mark takes my hand, and we step over the threshold. With my eyes fixed on the large living room, I can imagine myself in this house. The dining room full of friends. I picture children running up and down the stairs. Bread baking in the oven. Music. "Blue in Green."

Suddenly, I see myself reflected in Mom's face and I tremble. "We should adopt a dog," I say.

We go up to the second floor. I count each step. I want to memorize the path, the obstacles. We enter a sun-filled bedroom. From the window we can see the river. I keep my eyes open. I want to hold that scene.

"We should have a child," he says.

"I am going to finish my novel here," I reply.

I close my eyes. I no longer need movement. The motion is happening within me.

FORTY-NINE

I have lain awake for hours. I have a feeling I'll never move in with Mark. How many nights have I spent with him? Why did we go see a house in the suburbs? Everything has happened too fast, I think, and start to tremble. It's not out of fear, I tell myself. The bedroom is cold.

I study Mark as he sleeps and stroke him gently so as not to wake him. I climb out of bed and go over to the hall closet to grab a sweatshirt. In my mind, I hear Antonia's voice, an eternal prayer that hits me like the blow of a hammer: "You're rushing things. Don't move in with him."

Antonia, Antonia . . . it's like she's always there, watching me, protecting me. Some days Mark feels familiar; others, it's as if I am sleeping with a stranger. Antonia, I love him.

Occasionally, I pass the time opening and closing books from the shelf. What am I looking for? Mark has demonstrated that he loves me and for the first time I feel like I have a true friend. *Stop it, Leah!*

Looking down at the floor of the closet, I glimpse a white bag with a red stripe emerging from it but think nothing of it. I turn on a table lamp, plop down on the couch with my book, and snuggle into the cushions. For some reason I can't stop thinking about that red stripe. I walk back to the closet to examine the bag.

What are you doing, Leah? Haven't you overcome all your doubts by now? You are moving in together! The voices of my mother, Antonia, and Dr. Allen caution me against this sudden curiosity. But I am determined to find out what is in that bag in the closet, barely hidden behind boxes. I know I won't be able to sleep until I do so. I am awake, eyes wide open. I'm not living another one of my absurd nightmares.

The light makes the red appear orange. It is a woman's dress. I raise it to my nose to try to discover some smell, but fear is blocking my nostrils. My heart begins to race.

"It's Alice's dress," I whisper. I'm not dreaming this time. I am holding in my hands the proof that the red dress has not been a hallucination. There is no trace of lavender soap, nothing that connects it to Alice. I look for a stray hair that might provide a clue. I need to wake Mark up, confront him. What is this dress doing here? If I cry out, I am bound to wake him. I only have to cry out to return to reality. But what is reality?

I close my eyes and I can see Alice in this room, smiling. I open them and am alone.

When I close them, I once again feel observed.

Alice was here. Who does this apartment really belong to? And Michael? With my eyes closed, I see the three of them, laughing out loud in front of me.

I want to cry. . . . What should I do with the dress?

I grip the dress and feel something solid in the material. At last, some proof! I think. But do I need any more? Mark has deceived me. Alice deceived me. Mark and Alice . . .

I find a small piece of cardboard in one of the pockets of the dress. I feel it, my eyes tightly shut. I have no need to open them to know what I am holding. Overwhelmed with anguish, I feel this new certainty plunge me further: it is the daguerreotype of the blind girl.

FIFTY

More than a week has passed. Every night, before going to bed, I check that the red dress is still hidden behind the boxes in the closet. Every morning, I wake up with the hope that Mark will tell me his secret. Little by little, the smell of bergamot has begun to reemerge. It was the scent that brought me to him, but it is also a scent that I associate with death and fear, not the Mark I have come to know and love.

During the day, I avoid all contact with him, apart from a hug or a kiss. Each of us easily accepts the other's silence, like an old married couple who have lapsed into routine.

By Saturday night, I don't feel necessarily betrayed. I blame myself for having fallen into a trap and for not having the courage to ask him about it directly.

I avoid Mark's embrace as we climb into bed together for probably the last time. My exhaustion from so many sleepless nights has caught up with me, and I soon fall fast asleep.

Hours later, I am woken by a vibrating sound but pretend to be asleep. Maybe I ought to wake Mark, ask him to answer his phone. Maybe this call could put an end to my doubts. With my eyes shut, I follow his movements. Yes, he is getting up. Now he is sitting on the edge of the bed. He turns around to make sure I am still asleep. Then he answers his phone.

"Give me a second," he whispers, cautiously stepping out of bed.

He leaves the room and closes the door behind him. I am convinced he doesn't want me to hear the call. In fact, I think, I've noticed he has been uneasy and distant the entire day, regularly checking his messages.

I close my eyes and concentrate so that I can follow the sound of his movements: now he is out in the garden.

"I've been busy. I simply haven't had time," I hear him say. "No, I don't think we need to talk. What for? I haven't the slightest idea what you want." The pause is longer this time. Has he hung up? No, I'm convinced he is still holding the cell phone to his ear, that he is impatient. I can even make out his breathing.

"You're going to come here? Are you crazy?"

Who is it? I need to know, but Mark doesn't mention any name. His voice sounds both angry and anxious.

"All right, but not here. I'll see you on the subway platform in half an hour, and we can decide there. Yes, near the front of the train. And please, no more messages," he says with controlled fury, and ends the call.

The subway platform? It would take him ten, fifteen minutes to get there on foot. I hear him close the back door. I hear the sound of his breathing as he stands momentarily out in the hallway, with his hand on the doorknob. When he finally enters, I again pretend to be asleep.

I hear him rustle through the closet, gathering his shoes and jacket. He approaches me. I can feel his warmth, his breath. He kisses me gently on the cheek, pulls the quilt up over me, and stands beside the bed. He doesn't want to leave, he doesn't want to abandon me. He kisses me again, this time on my brow. He pauses in the doorway and looks at me one last time. Head bowed, trying to avoid the slightest noise, he opens the front door and goes out into the street.

As soon as I hear the door close, I make a mental map of how to reach the train station. I am determined to confront my enemy, whoever it might be. I will need to turn right and walk for three blocks. On the corner, turn left.

Going over this trajectory in my mind, I put on the red dress quickly, pick up my bag, and leave the apartment I've shared with Mark, guided by the smell of bergamot.

I step onto the sidewalk, tapping my stick to find my way. I must keep my eyes closed to keep my senses sharp. By now I've gotten the hang of navigating the cracks in the narrow sidewalks and the potholes at the corners of the streets.

The smell of bergamot is still guiding me and I feel it getting sharper, more acidic, more biting. By my calculation, he must already be at the Hoyt-Schermerhorn subway station.

The slight drizzle in the air disorients me. A police car is keeping pace with me. The car comes to a halt. I hear the door slam and hasty footsteps coming in my direction. I stop walking.

"Do you need help, miss?" a gruff-voiced officer asks. He must have watched me stumble.

"Are you lost?" he insists, this time in a gentler tone.

I don't have time for this. But I know that if I don't answer the officer, I'll only be delayed further.

"Just headed to the subway, thanks," I say, tapping with my stick. "Yes, the station's on the corner, I can tell."

"I don't think it's a good idea to be out walking around here at this time of night. If you're going to the station, I'll accompany you."

"I'm almost there, thanks. Don't worry." I hear the man walk back to his patrol car and start the engine. He drives slowly alongside me until I reach the station entrance. I wave and enter.

I slide my card through the slot, hear the turnstile rotate. I walk silently down the steps and hear voices on the platform.

I open my eyes. He is here with a woman. First image: the two of them, standing face-to-face. Second image: she has reached up and is cupping his face with both hands, searching. Third image: he's stepped back, a finger pointed at her.

"She believed you," are the first words I am able to distinguish. Mark is speaking quietly yet forcefully, as if trying not to make a scene. Though there is no one here but the three of us.

He is talking about me. And the woman he is talking to is Alice. "What have we become?" It's Alice's voice. My nightmare is back.

FIFTY-ONE

Hidden on the staircase landing, I can hear more clearly now.

"I've loved you ever since that god-awful theater group when you dreamed of becoming an actress. Then you left me for Michael and his money. Until that wasn't enough for you. Then you decided you wanted me again, but you wanted everything else too. Just look at what you've unleashed."

"Oh, so now it's my fault, is it, Mark?"

He is Mark. He's always been Mark, my Mark.

"When I moved to Mont Cenis, you were the one who recognized the building. You knew my neighbor was blind, you knew her story. You were her friend at the bookstore. And it was you who took out the baseboards in the hallway so that my voice would filter through. So that she would hear everything. Have you forgotten that already? You were the one who made it all possible, not me. It was all so we could be together."

"My only intention was to save you from Michael."

"Michael could've killed me."

"But we ended up killing Michael."

"Leah killed Michael—that wasn't part of the plan."

"Then, I'm the only one to blame."

Silence.

"What now? Why are you quiet?"

Silence.

"The only thing we needed was a blind witness," Alice says. "Michael wasn't going to suspect a girl who couldn't see or fend for herself. He never imagined she'd be the witness of his abuse."

I want to get Mark away from Alice, away from the story she is telling him. Now I can see Mark without his hat. The smell of bergamot in my bedroom . . . in the hallway . . . in the elevator.

"But Michael started going after her. You saw that creepy daguerreotype she left in the mailbox. He must have been the one trolling her on Instagram," Mark says. "I never thought this would end up with your husband dead."

His voice . . . Poor Mark . . .

"Neither did I!" Alice shouts. "We only wanted her to witness a case of domestic violence. But then she showed up with that damned knife!"

I imagine Alice trembling, her lovely eyes on the ground. Poor Alice . . .

That's right: I'm the guilty one. I'm the murderer. I don't feel any pain or hatred or guilt. It is over. I finally know the truth. This was their lovers' game, and I was nothing but a pawn in it. I turn around to leave, disappear forever. But then Mark speaks again.

"You made Michael take up drinking again, Alice. You said he was abusive, but he'd never laid a finger on you."

"He *was* abusive, Mark!" I hear Alice's voice crack with despair. "He nearly killed Leah and me that day, coming back from Woodstock. If he'd known about you, he would've finished you. And you know it too. How was I supposed to get away from him? Move back to Springfield? Kill myself? You know I came close to it."

I cling to the filthy handrail, not daring to go down the last steps and confront them on the platform.

"Mark, it's too late now. We can't go back. Now, you have to get rid of her. I know Leah. This isn't going to end well."

But it will end the way it's supposed to. The way I've known it would all along. Like Mrs. Orman. I remember her face still flushed from that last fight with her husband ten years ago. The tears still on her cheeks. Poor Mrs. Orman, I couldn't see her suffer anymore. I was only eighteen years old. How could I let her continue to live in such agony? With my eyes closed, I gave her what she asked me for: a gentle push out the window.

I told Mom, Dr. Allen, Antonia, Mrs. Elman, and Olivia what I did—why wouldn't I?

I had been with Mrs. Orman at her darkest moment and helped her escape her husband's abuse. But according to them, my help was the sign of a mental breakdown. Until Michael Turner, I've kept all other acts of charity to myself. In the case of his death, I had no other choice but to follow orders.

"Alice, Leah and I want to make a life together," I hear him say.

"You can't fool me, Mark. You're doing this for her money. Be honest, that's why you got back together with me as well, for whatever we might get from my husband."

"No, Alice. I love her. This is the chance to make amends for all the evil we've done. When she turned up at my apartment all those weeks ago . . ."

Mark loves me. I begin to tremble; my eyes fill with tears. I can no longer tell what is real or not. In my stories, Mark and I are together. But the truth is, I've lived all my life alone. It didn't matter that he was by my side, I lived alone. At Mont Cenis with my father or my mother or Antonia, I've always been alone. I'm sure of that. As sure as I was when I pressed the pillow down on my mother's face. The air in her hospice room was heavy with dry sweat, damp sheets, and urine. Guilt had fed on her for years. Cancer, for months. After what she did to me. After all she did for me, I couldn't bear to see her suffer. Poor Mom . . . She needed my help. And I noticed she was smiling when I approached her and I didn't blink so that I could hold on to that last image, somehow happy, knowing that I was saving her. One last breath and that was it.

"You have to get rid of her," Alice repeats.

"I don't have to do anything, Alice. Stop calling me," Mark says.

The blast from the train whistle drowns out their voices. I shudder, as if the locomotive is bearing down on me.

"I loved you," Mark continues. "It took me a while to realize you were only using me. And you manipulated Leah even more. It's unforgivable. Everything you did was for money. And then you up and left."

They did it for Money. I did it for mercy and protection. That's all I ever do. Like the last night I had dinner with Olivia and Mrs. Elman. From my blazer pocket, I pulled out one of the small glass bottles from my medicine cabinet. One of Antonia's sacred potions. Drops to calm anxiety, drops for energy, drops for good luck, drops to lower and raise blood pressure.

One drop, another, one more. I emptied three full droppers into the lace handkerchief I was sure Mrs. Elman would place over her mouth and nose once she got a whiff of the tincture's alluring combination of chamomile, mint, cardamom, and cinnamon. It hurt me to see her go. But it was time; she was old. It was a slow, soothing way to die.

First the tea, which I made for her, and then the handkerchief. A sweet goodbye. When you reach ninety and you're dragging your feet and need help to get up and sit down, to lie down, to bathe, to sleep, even to eat, what is the meaning of life? Olivia could no longer carry that burden. Poor Mrs. Elman. Olivia too suffered so much at the end. I regret that I wasn't there to help. Poor Olivia.

"You knew I had to leave the city, if not the country. That was part of our plan as well. Then I was supposed to come back for you, which is what I'm doing now. Do you not remember any of this? What's happened to you? It's like you're in another world."

Alice reaches out to touch his face again, but he takes a step backward, away from her. Through gritted teeth, he says: "Get away from me."

"You have to leave her. You can't go on seeing her, Mark. Don't you get it? Can't you see the mess you're getting us into?"

Antonia was never the same again after that first heart attack. High blood pressure, swollen legs, jaundiced eyes, poor mobility. Poor Antonia . . . one, two, three, four Boston ivy seeds, ground and stirred into her teacup, lowered her blood pressure until it was nothing, and her pain was gone forever.

"This is my chance to start over. To make a life with Leah. I have a right to."

"You feel guilty, you feel sorry for her." Pleading, Alice tries to take hold of his forearms, but he takes a step to the right to avoid her.

"No, Alice. I love her. And I'm not going back. My life is with her." His voice softens. "We're living together."

"Oh, Mark!"

We're living together? Now we're just sleeping together. Now he desires me and I desire him. Soon we will live together, Mark and I. We will have a house outside the city, near the Hudson river.

He is looking down at the train tracks now as if hypnotized.

"Mark!" Alice cries out again. "You're living with her?"

"Yes, Alice. Leah and I are living together."

Yes, we will adopt a dog, plant flowers in the garden, paint the house in light colors.

"Mark, where is Leah right now? Where did you leave her?" Alice shouts, her whole body shaking.

"At home. Don't worry, she was sound asleep when I left. I don't think she's going to wake up. But that's why I must get back. It's late. I don't want her to be on her own."

Stunned, I lean back against the wall near the staircase.

"When we spoke . . ." she starts, but the noise of the oncoming train forces her to repeat her question: "Where was Leah when you answered the phone?"

"I told you, asleep in our bedroom."

"And where were you? Where were you speaking from, Mark?"

"From outside, with the door closed. There's no way she could have heard me."

Alice raises her hand to her mouth in horror. "Mark," she shouts hysterically. "Leah can hear voices from far away. Leah heard you. She hears *everything.*"

"Blue in Green" was playing when Mom and I got home the night of my eighth birthday. I see it all so clearly now. The night before, I had made a potion and slipped it in his glass, to help him feel less sad; I had seen Antonia prepare the mixture before. But it didn't work. He was feverish and in a rage. Mad at Mom for wanting to leave him. Hating himself for failing at everything. At one point, he swung his fist out to hit her, but he hit me instead. It was an accident. I had rushed between them to stop them from fighting.

"It won't happen again, I promise," said Mom, as we hugged each other and cried, unable to sleep. That night we locked ourselves in the room. We heard him slam the door. Where had Dad gone? Poor Dad . . .

"Tomorrow is your birthday and you and I will celebrate it alone."

"And what will happen with Dad?" I asked, afraid.

"Dad is sick," she said, and I felt like she was swallowing hard.

On my birthday we went to the theater. I know why I don't remember anything about *The Lion King*: I spent the entire night thinking of Dad. I was scared. I knew that when we returned, late at night, he might hit Mom again.

When we reached the building, Mom waited for the elevator and I dashed up the stairs. I opened the door and the long hallway was dark. I entered, quietly, avoiding making the slightest noise. The whole apartment was dark but I could see a dim thread of amber light coming from underneath the closed bathroom door.

I drew near, trying to hear him, but could only make out his heavy breathing.

I placed my hand on the doorknob and carefully opened the door. First I saw his bare feet on the ground. With the door wide open, I saw my father with a syringe buried in a vein in his left arm.

Like a beast, he got up and screamed, "Get out of here! Go away!" The syringe fell to the ground and a stream of blood ran down his arm.

I was static; I couldn't react. I closed my eyes, I started to shiver, and I felt my dad's bloodstained hand on my neck. He tightened his grip; I couldn't breathe. I made no effort to free myself from him. I remained there, at a standstill. Slowly, I felt his hand relax until it was no longer squeezing me; it was more like a caress. Whatever he had injected was taking effect, and his heart was pounding as if it was going to give in. When he let go of me, I fell against the glass shelf, which rained down on top of me. The noise of the glass bottle falling to the floor and breaking made me shudder. I felt my skin was about to crack, as if I had turned into glass. My arm burned as if I had cut myself. Now the smell of bergamot was everywhere; the blood was his and mine.

In his anguish, he curled up on the bathroom floor. I saw him shiver, cry, but he didn't have the energy to speak. What did he inject into his arm? How many drops had he taken from the amber jars that Antonia kept in the medicine cabinet? How much whiskey did he drink from the bottle? Accidental overdose, they said. Overdose? Everyone chooses their own destiny. Dad chose his.

Poor Dad . . . I opened my eyes and he was in front of me. I saw he had a long, sharp piece of glass in his right hand. I understood what Dad wanted to do. Now I saw him with the sharp end of the glass close to his left arm, which was still spurting blood. He wanted to open his wound, bleed out once and for all, I thought.

I approached him. I sat in front of him, real close. His lips tried to move, they trembled. "Help me," he babbled.

He had lost all his strength and was unable to press the sharp glass against his arm.

I took the hand gripping the glass and I moved it up to his neck. He aimed the long and thin bloodstained tip to his neck, to his throat. I helped him. He asked me for help. Poor Dad . . . I tried with all my might to get the glass to pierce him. One more blow, a push. In that instant, my father recovered, and with the last strength he had in him, he helped me get the glass to pierce him. Everything happened in a few seconds.

His blood began to cover me. The smell of rust and bergamot became increasingly intense. I heard the apartment door open.

"Leah!" my mother screamed.

I heard the next scream come from inside the bathroom. When she saw me crouched over my father, I saw the terror in her eyes. She grabbed my arm and tried to help me up, and now I was the one who was drained of strength.

In one fell swoop, my mother picked me up but I slipped on the bloody floor. I felt my head hit the edge of the toilet and never woke up again.

Was I dead? When I opened my eyes in the hospital, the world had stopped before me. I was the only one spinning.

Antonia tried as hard as she could to scrub away my memory, to keep me from feeling any pain. Mom gave her life away for my sake; Dr. Allen tried his best to help me learn how to understand and live with my condition. But I could never see my way out of it. What I need now is a cure. Or oblivion.

The train is pulling into the station. I rush down the remaining stairs and come to a halt on the last step. I see Alice look in my direction, recognize the red dress. Mark's back is to me. I take a step forward and nearly stumble. I grab the handrail for support and blink.

First image: Alice standing on the yellow line at the platform edge, staring wide-eyed at me. Second image: Alice leaned over, clutching at Mark's arm, with a look of horror on her face as her body topples toward the rails. Mark turns, sees me and fixes his eyes on my belly. Poor Alice, poor Mark . . . In that instant, I run to them, stretch out my arms to reach them, but they lose their balance and fall into the void. Third image: Alice and Mark, their bodies frozen in midair in front of the train that will hit them.

I blink again several times. The train driver sounds the whistle. I remain rooted to my spot near the stairs, still with my hands on my stomach. I am pregnant, I am sure of it. I will have a girl. She will have white-blond hair and wear white lace dresses.

The scent of iron and rust overtakes me. The sound of metal on metal brings me to my knees. I look up and can clearly distinguish several people running toward me.

The driver emerges from his cab, a look of horror on his face.

"Oh my God!" he shouts. "It was an accident! I couldn't stop—they came out of nowhere."

A few alarmed passengers begin to appear on the platform, looking like bewildered ghosts. Their cries are like an echo of despair as they hurry past me. Moment by moment, the smell of rust and iron begins to fade. So do all the other smells: I am gradually losing them.

I let my white stick fall and watch with complete and utter fascination as it rolls to the yellow line marking the danger zone. Balancing for a second on the edge of the platform, it falls into the abyss and vanishes.

I can see movement. My eyes are wide open.

ACKNOWLEDGMENTS

The Silence in Her Eyes is a novel that I wanted to write for many years. The first person I told about the idea was Johanna Castillo, who was then my editor at Atria Books, Simon & Schuster, and is now my literary agent. When we writers try to work on a book that is a departure from what we are known for, we often don't get much encouragement. I began to work on the novel in secret. Then the pandemic arrived and that confinement gave me time to finish *The Silence in Her Eyes*. When Johanna read the first draft of the manuscript, she was thrilled.

The first thanks goes to her for trusting my ideas and seeing potential in them.

To Sarah Branham, who patiently read my manuscript, made many recommendations, and polished Nick Caistor and Faye Williams's excellent translation.

To Cecilia Molinari, my friend, who always gets me out of trouble when I need several pages translated into English in a matter of hours sometimes.

To Libby McGuire, Jonathan Karp, and especially Daniella Wexler, who acquired the novel for Atria Books.

To Peter Borland, my great editor for his precise eye, for his care-

ACKNOWLEDGMENTS

ful work with my texts. I can no longer see myself writing with any editor other than Peter.

When I became almost obsessively involved with the story of Leah and her akinetopsia, my family and friends had to put up with me telling them the tribulations of a woman who could not see movement. Thanks to Mirta Ojito, Laura Bryant, Romy Verité, Ovidio Rodríguez, Verónica Cervera, and Cristobal Pera, who with their comments and readings guided me along this solitary path.

To my mother, my first reader.

To Gonzalo, Emma, Anna, and Lucas, who I hope will read this novel someday. Anna, by the way, was the inspiration for Leah's eyes.